LOVING THE UNEXPECTED EARL

Romancing the Ton, Book 2

Christina Diane

ARE YOU SIGNED UP FOR DRAGONBLADE'S BLOG?

You'll get the latest news and information on exclusive giveaways, exclusive excerpts, coming releases, sales, free books, cover reveals and more.

Check out our complete list of authors, too!

No spam, no junk. That's a promise!

Sign Up Here

www.dragonbladepublishing.com

Dearest Reader;

Thank you for your support of a small press. At Dragonblade Publishing, we strive to bring you the highest quality Historical Romance from some of the best authors in the business. Without your support, there is no 'us', so we sincerely hope you adore these stories and find some new favorite authors along the way.

Happy Reading!

CEO, Dragonblade Publishing

Additional Dragonblade books by Author Christina Diane

Romancing the Ton Series
Avoiding the Merry Viscount (Book 1)
Loving the Unexpected Earl (Book 2)

Dragonblade Anthologies
Dukes All Night Long

Dedication

For all of you who know there's something irresistible about an honorable, inexperienced earl who loses himself…in his breeches.

Note to Readers

Thank you so much for picking up my book—I'm truly delighted (and doing an undignified happy dance) that you're here!

Before we step into the historical world of Christina Diane, I wanted to share a little something about what to expect. While my books are set in the Regency era, I write with the modern reader in mind. You can expect stories that are character-driven, fast-paced, and heavy on the spice, with lively dialogue and plenty of heart.

I do my best to capture the setting and language of the time through research, but strict historical accuracy isn't my primary goal. Sometimes my characters insist on doing and speaking things their own way—and I let them. So, if you're looking for meticulous period detail and perfect historical precision, this book may not be what you are looking for (and that's completely okay!).

But if you're here for passionate heroines, swoonworthy gentlemen, witty banter, high stakes, high heat, and happily-ever-afters, all wrapped in a Regency-inspired world that welcomes diverse, bold, and intriguing characters—you're in the right place.

I hope this story sweeps you off your feet and carries you into a world of romance, tension, and a touch of scandal.

Much love and swoon,

Content Warnings

This book doesn't dive deep into the dark stuff—but you might encounter boundary-challenged relatives, oversharing friends, and a generous dash of spice. I aim to flag anything that might need a warning to ensure a safe reading experience for all. But if I miss something, send me a message so I can update the list for future readers. To keep this message spoiler-free, you can check out identified content warnings here: christinadianebooks.com/content-warnings

CHAPTER ONE

Graham

Early Spring, 1812
Mayfair
London, England

GRAHAM TUGGED AT his cravat for the third time in as many minutes. His entire world had been turned upside down, resulting in his attendance at the first ball of the London Season. Every second since he arrived, he fought the urge to bolt from the stuffy ballroom like a timid colt. The crystal chandeliers threw dancing shadows across marble floors that probably cost more than most men earned in a lifetime. And the eyes fixed on him everywhere he looked caused his calloused palms to sweat inside his evening gloves.

Just days ago, he had been preparing for colt season at his home in the country, where he bred and raised horses. And now, here he was, the new Earl of Powis, and every person in this ballroom knew he didn't belong. He hadn't been born among this set, and he could assume he only received an invitation so the whole of society might have something to talk about in their drawing rooms.

He shouldn't have agreed to attend, but after the tense visit from Silas Rothwell this morning, it would benefit him to make more connections. At least that was what Matt said. Graham wasn't certain he agreed now that he'd entered the lion's den.

Forty-five thousand pounds. That was the sum of the gambling debts his dissolute cousin left for Graham to deal with.

"You look ready to flee," Matt observed, appearing at his elbow with two glasses of champagne. "Drink this. It will help."

Graham accepted the glass gratefully. Matt, the Earl of Wilton, had been his salvation these past weeks. They had been friends of sorts when Matt was his customer, stocking his stables with the fine horseflesh that Graham had raised alongside his cousin.

"I hope you have more where this came from," Graham jested, taking a healthy swallow of champagne. "Because I'm quite unequipped to navigate all of this."

"You managed to build the finest horse breeding operation in England," Matt said firmly. "You can manage this. Half of these peacocks couldn't manage a profitable estate if their lives depended on it."

He wasn't certain he could manage a profitable estate either. Especially once he determined what he had to do to raise the funds to pay Rothwell. Raising horses and running estates weren't exactly the same thing. And now he wouldn't even get to work with the horses anymore. Men of his station didn't "work," so the business would be fully in John's hands while Graham did whatever it was that an earl did.

And unfortunately, his business didn't earn enough money to pay the debt. And letting his mother or his cousin know about his situation was the last thing he wished to do.

It had only been a week since he had found out about the unexpected inheritance, so he was mostly learning as he went. His education started with etiquette and dance instruction that Matt had insisted on. Matt wasn't aware that he had far bigger problems than how he carried himself in society. But he took his friend's advice, deciding it was better to have a friend. And even with the lessons, he would stay as far away from the dance floor as possible if he had anything to say about it.

He ran his hand through his hair, catching himself in the nervous gesture his mother had always chided him for. But she was settled back in Sussex, sending him to face the wolves alone. He assumed she would prefer to remain in hiding there. His father's constant dance with scandal in the form of affairs and dalliances, had taught her long ago to avoid society's scrutiny.

"Come," Matt said, placing a steady hand on Graham's shoulder. "I want you to meet some good friends of mine. These men have been looking forward to an introduction."

They moved through the crowd, Graham conscious of heads turning and whispered tittering all around them. Everyone knew the previous Earl of Powis had been a dissolute wastrel. They were all waiting to see if the new earl would follow suit.

If only they knew how far from the truth that was. Graham had sworn off his father's libertine path years ago, after watching what such behavior cost the women left behind. Especially his mother.

"Elias," Matt called as they approached a group alongside a nearby wall. "Allow me to present the Earl of Powis. Graham, meet Viscount Snowdon."

The viscount was a pleasant-faced man with kind eyes and an easy smile. He extended his hand to Graham. "Powis, a pleasure. I've heard a lot about you. Any friend of Matt's is welcome among us."

"Thank you, my lord. I'm grateful for the introduction." Graham meant it. These few moments of normal conversation made him feel far less alone.

"Hudson Brooks, Earl of Onslow," another voice joined them, though the tone carried less warmth. Graham turned to face a dark-haired man whose sharp gaze burned through him.

"Lord Onslow." Graham inclined his head politely.

"So you're a friend of Wilton's?" Hudson didn't seem as if he actually intended for Graham to answer the question. "I'll assume that your character is far superior to his and do my best to overlook the association."

The insult was clearly aimed at Matt. Graham glanced between the two men, noting the tension that crackled between them. Matt's jaw tightened, but he maintained his composure.

"Always a pleasure, Onslow," Matt said with forced cheer. "I see you're in your usual charming mood."

"My mood was well enough before you made your presence known," Hudson replied coldly.

Elias cleared his throat. "Hudson, we've all been friends since we were boys. Can you just for one night—"

"I believe I am expected to dance with my sister for this set." Hudson glared at Matt's face. Then he refocused his attention on Graham. "Powis, welcome to London. Do let me know if you need advice from an honorable man." With that parting shot, he stalked away.

Graham watched him go, then turned to Matt. "Good God, what was that about?"

"Hudson being Hudson," Matt answered, draining half his champagne in one go. "The man holds grudges like a child collecting sweets. Don't give it another thought. Come, let me introduce you to the others in our set."

Before they could move, a shrill voice cut through their conversation. "Lord Powis!" A formidable woman in purple silk bore down on them, a simpering blonde daughter in tow. "Lady Pemberton. I simply must introduce you to my dear Clarissa."

Not another one.

"Ah," Matt murmured, "you can't take a single step unnoticed by these vipers."

Graham felt trapped as Lady Pemberton launched into a detailed recitation of her daughter's accomplishments, which seemed to consist primarily of playing the pianoforte and speaking passable French. Clarissa giggled at inappropriate intervals and batted her eyelashes so frequently Graham wondered if she had something in her eye.

"Perhaps you might call on us tomorrow?" Lady Pemberton concluded with obvious hope.

"I'm afraid I have pressing estate business," Graham managed, praying that the excuse would free him from an afternoon in their company.

"Of course, of course. Such responsibilities you must have! Perhaps next week then?"

Matt stepped smoothly forward. "Lady Pemberton, you must excuse us. Lord Powis promised to accompany me to the smoking room to tell the men about his magnificent horses."

"Oh." Lady Pemberton's face fell. "Of course. Just know that you can call on us anytime. Cook's lemon cakes are the best you'll ever taste."

It wasn't the first lemon cake he'd been offered that evening, and he could be certain it wasn't the last.

Matt nodded to the woman and ushered Graham away. Once they had escaped, Graham sighed. "What would I do without you?"

"Don't worry," Matt said with a grin. "I've had years of practice dodging matchmaking mothers. Stay close to me and I'll run interference. You can't ever let them catch you alone."

"Is this what every social event will be like?"

"Until you're either married or deemed a disreputable rake, yes. Though I must say, watching you navigate the marriage mart is rather entertaining."

"And what if I don't aim for either?" Graham glanced around the ballroom, noting several other mothers eyeing him with predatory interest. "Perhaps we should find somewhere less conspicuous to stand. We seem to be more like sitting ducks."

"This dance is ending, so I can introduce you to Elias and Hudson's sisters and their friends." Matt led him to where the men he'd just met had joined a group of beautiful women stood in animated conversation. "The first one there is Diana...Elias's sister."

Graham's gaze found her immediately. Golden hair caught the light from the candles, and her blue gown complemented her coloring perfectly. When she turned slightly, he caught her profile. She was breathtaking. It wasn't just her heart-shaped face with deep dimples that made her beautiful, but the way she appeared determined when she spoke.

She was everything he was not—confident, clearly comforta-ble in this world he was still learning to navigate. And there was something about her that tightened his chest that was unlike anything he'd ever experienced.

"She's…" He couldn't finish the thought without sounding like a fool.

"Come," Matt said. "I'll make the introduction."

They approached the group, and as they drew closer, she turned. Their eyes met, and something shifted inside Graham.

Her eyes were sapphire blue, and when she looked at him, it was with a kindness and curiosity that he didn't dare look away from.

"Diana," Matt said with obvious affection, "allow me to present the Earl of Powis. Powis, Lady Diana Armstrong."

She curtsied gracefully, and when she rose, those sapphire eyes met his with warmth. "Lord Powis, what a pleasure to—"

"Oh how wonderful!" Another voice interrupted as a woman in emerald green swept toward them, a pale brown-haired daughter trailing eagerly behind. "Lord Powis! Lady Weatherby, and this is my darling Amelia. We simply must—"

"Lady Weatherby," Diana said smoothly, stepping slightly closer to Graham, "how lovely to see you. My brother asked me to make sure Lord Powis attends him directly on a matter of importance." She smiled apologetically. "Perhaps you might catch his lordship later in the evening?"

Lady Weatherby's face fell, but she couldn't argue with such polite deflection. "Of course, Lady Diana. We look forward to speaking with you, my lord."

As the woman retreated, Diana turned back to Graham with a satisfied expression.

"That was smoothly done," Graham said, surprised to find himself genuinely amused. "Do you make a habit of rescuing gentlemen in need?"

"Well I am quite good at it, it would seem," she teased, her adorable deep dimples on full display as she smiled up at him.

"I had better remain close to you then. If the events of the evening have been any indication, I am certain I will require the services of a beautiful knight on a white horse to come to my aid."

She released a laugh that sounded like the tinkling of bells. "Perhaps not on a horse, but I'll take that as a compliment."

"Do you not enjoy horses?"

Wouldn't that be his luck: to meet an enchanting woman, only to learn that she despised horses?

"I adore them," she answered quickly. "I just never learned to ride." She glanced toward her brother and then back to Graham. "I'm not allowed."

The admission caught him off guard. "Not allowed? By whom?"

"My father." Her voice carried a note of frustration that she quickly tried to mask. "He forbade it after my mother died in a riding accident when I was eight. Elias can't even ride a horse in his presence."

Graham felt something twist in his chest at the sadness that flickered across her features. "I'm sorry for your loss. It must have been difficult to lose your mother at such a young age."

He wasn't that much older than her when he lost his father. But he wouldn't allow any thoughts of his father to ruin what had become the most intriguing conversation he'd had since he'd arrived in London.

"Thank you." She lifted her chin slightly, and he could see the effort she put into composing herself. "But enough about that. Tell me, what have you found most surprising since you have joined us here in London?"

"Surprising? The sheer number of lemon cakes I've been promised tonight. Evidently, the single greatest weapon among the matchmakers is in their baked goods."

Her dimples flashed as she laughed. "It could be worse. You might be promised pianoforte recitals instead of pastries. Those, I assure you, last much longer and are far less satisfying."

He couldn't help but grin like a school boy at the clever woman before him. "A fair point. I shall certainly run the other direction."

"That shall only make them chase you harder, I'm afraid."

"And here I thought it was the women who preferred to be chased."

Her eyes sparkled with mischief, and everything around them fell away. All he could focus on was her.

"Ah," she started, "but perhaps we prefer to let men think they are the hunters, when really we've been leading them all along."

Her words caught him off guard, clever and bold in a way he hadn't expected. He should have laughed, offered some reply, but instead he found himself studying the curve of her smile and the way her eyes glinted with challenge.

The moment stretched, charged with something he couldn't quite define. He tried to form coherent thoughts as he scrambled for a witty reply.

"Powis," Matt called to him, breaking through the moment, "Lady Harrowby is approaching. She's the one I warned you about."

He did his best to hide his irritation at their conversation being interrupted. Graham glanced up at an imposing older woman in diamonds and an impressive number of feathers in her turban moving with purpose in their direction.

"Brace yourself," Diana murmured with amusement.

"Lady Harrowby," Matt said as the woman reached them, "It's lovely to see you as always. May I present the Earl of Powis?"

Graham bowed over the lady's gloved hand. "A pleasure to meet you, your ladyship."

She studied him with sharp eyes that seemed to see everything. "So you're the new Powis. I knew your cousin, you know. Dreadful man. I trust you'll be an improvement."

"I certainly hope so, my lady."

Something about the woman made him straighten up out of fear. Matt was correct in his assessment that the woman was nothing short of a dragon.

"Hmm." She continued her assessment. "At least you have proper manners. That's more than could be said for him." Her gaze shifted to Diana. "And I see you've already met our dear Diana. Excellent judge of character, that one. If she can tolerate your conversation, you can't be entirely hopeless."

She looked him up and down and then continued on her way, waving her hand toward them as she passed. "Enjoy your evening."

"Did I just pass some sort of test?" he asked, leaning closer than he should have to Diana. The scent of lavender radiating from her did little to ease his desire to move even closer.

"She never stops testing any of us," Diana said with obvious amusement.

Before Graham could respond, a new voice interrupted them. "Lady Diana?"

They turned to see a tall, raven-haired gentleman standing before them, extending his arm to Diana. He was impeccably dressed and carried himself with the easy assurance of someone who had never questioned his place in the world.

"Lord Ockham," Diana said, taking his arm.

Her blue eyes didn't seem to sparkle the same way that they had when she was speaking with him. But she didn't appear unhappy to see the man either, which grated on his nerves. A realization that he refused to explore any further.

"I believe this is our dance," Ockham said to her.

"Indeed it is. I've been looking forward to a chance to speak with you."

Did she have some kind of understanding with the man? Was she already spoken for? Not that it should affect Graham in any way. He couldn't consider the notion of courtship with the debts he faced. They'd call him a fortune hunter and only after a woman for her dowry. And he had promised himself long ago that he'd marry for love. But regardless of his situation, he still didn't enjoy the idea of her being courted by another man.

Ockham's gaze shifted briefly to Graham, assessing. "Powis, isn't it? I heard you'd arrived in town."

"Good to meet you, Lord Ockham." Graham inclined his head, using all of his control to fight the irrational surge of irritation coursing through him.

"I hope to see you at our club soon," Ockham replied. His tone was almost friendly, which only irritated Graham more. The man nodded toward the floor. "I believe the dance is about to begin."

Diana glanced back at Graham, and he caught what might have been reluctance in her expression. Or perhaps that was just what he wanted to see.

"It was a pleasure meeting you, Lord Powis. I do hope we'll have occasion to speak again."

"The pleasure was entirely mine, Lady Diana."

As Ockham led her toward the dance floor, Graham watched them for a moment, noting how easily Diana moved with the other man, how right they appeared together. More so than she would with a horse breeder turned earl who faced the wrong end of a pistol if he didn't pay off the lowlife his cousin owed money to.

He tried to force himself to look away, but then her eyes found his. And in that reckless moment he forgot the debt, the danger, the noose tightening around his neck. A man could lose everything to a look like that from a woman who was unlike any that he'd ever met.

And he suspected he was about to.

CHAPTER TWO
Diana

DIANA BIT BACK a satisfied grin as Lord Ockham led her from the dance floor, their conversation still fresh in her mind. The dance with the man had been what she'd hoped. He was genuinely interested in discussing estate management. She had planted seeds of her knowledge after she'd heard that his estates may not be performing well after his father's passing.

When he'd mentioned the challenges he faced, she'd offered insights about crop rotation strategies, and he'd actually listened. It was rare to find a man who would take a woman's advice on such matters. And for the first time all evening, she'd felt useful.

Other than when she'd rescued Lord Powis. She certainly hadn't expected him to be as captivating as he was. It was no surprise that he'd be the catch of the season. If he wished to marry, that is.

There had been something genuine about Lord Powis that she hadn't expected. Most men of the *ton* carried themselves with learned arrogance, but he'd seemed almost... grateful for her intervention. And those green eyes had looked at her as if he truly saw her, not just another eligible lady. The thought was both thrilling and terrifying. But Lord Powis was clearly overwhelmed by London society, and she couldn't build a practical future on fleeting attraction.

"Thank you for the dance, Lady Diana," Lord Ockham said as they reached the edge of the ballroom where her friends were. "I hope we might continue our conversation, as I have a few more questions. Might I call on you sometime?"

She beamed at the compliment. And how well her plan had come together. He met all of her requirements for a practical match. He was handsome and kind, allowing her to put her knowledge into practice.

She'd read every book on agriculture and modern farming practices she could find after she'd been replaced as the lady of their household. Her brother had unexpectedly married for love, and that meant Lydia was responsible for their household. A responsibility that had fallen to Diana from an early age. She wanted to remain useful, and embroidery would never be enough to occupy her time or her mind.

"I would enjoy that very much, my lord."

"I hope you enjoy the rest of your evening. I believe I might take in a bit of fresh air."

As he bowed and took his leave, Diana watched him disappear into the crowd. She would enjoy the conversation very much, but she wasn't certain she overly enjoyed the company of that particular man. There certainly wasn't any measurable attraction beyond the superficial nature.

It was unlike the unexpected flutter she'd felt when Lord Powis had leaned close enough for her to catch the scent of his cologne and spot the gold flecks in his green eyes. But Ockham could offer her what she wanted. Notions of love and unrelenting attraction just weren't on her list of requirements.

"Diana!" Hannah exclaimed, clasping her arm and pulling her closer. "How did it go with Lord Ockham?"

Diana glanced at the four women who had become her closest friends who were more like family, truth be told. Hannah Brooks had been her closest friend since childhood and knew everything there was to know about her. Then there was the sharp-witted gossip, Tabitha Parker, whose auburn curls never seemed to stay properly pinned. Juliana Gordon—now Viscountess Gordon after her marriage last season—was the most kind and generous person Diana had ever met, while one could tell what Marina Osborne was thinking from the moment they looked at her. And currently, Marina was fanning herself with obvious irritation.

"It was perfectly pleasant," Diana said, accepting a glass of lemonade from a passing footman.

"Pleasant?" Tabitha raised an eyebrow. "That's all?"

Diana shrugged. "We discussed estate management, and he actually listened to my suggestions about how he could improve crop yields."

Marina snapped her fan shut. "And you believe this to be an indicator that you should encourage a courtship with the man?"

"Marina," Hannah chided gently, though her eyes held concern. "Diana, are you certain Lord Ockham is really for you?"

Diana bit her lip. "What do you mean? He's perfectly respectable. Handsome, titled, and clearly in need of a wife who could assist with his estates."

"Diana, do you truly want a marriage focused on crops and livestock instead of love or even friendship?"

The question stung more than Diana cared to admit. "I must marry someday. And if I can be useful—"

"But what about happiness?" Marina interrupted. "What about feeling your heart race when you lay eyes on the man, or longing to hear his voice?"

Diana glanced around the ballroom, spying Lord Powis again. She had watched him when she was dancing with Ockham, too. There was just something about the man.

He stood near the refreshment table with Lord Wilton, and even from across the room, she could see the tension in his shoulders. There was a vulnerability to him that made her want to smooth away his worries.

Then she forced herself to look away. "Love is a luxury for those who have the time to wait for it. I need to make a good match this season. I'm twenty years old, and even Elias managed to marry before I did. None of us ever thought that would happen. I'm just wasting time."

"Wasting time?" Hannah's voice rose slightly. "Diana, you're hardly on the shelf."

"Perhaps not. But Elias and Papa have no need of my help, and neither does Lydia. I want to be useful. Where my presence matters."

"You matter to us," Tabitha said softly.

"Of course, but that's different. And eventually, we're all going to marry."

Diana touched her mother's diamond necklace, wishing that she were there to guide her. "I am tired of waiting for something that may never be. And if I can find a comfortable marriage where I can focus my time on something I enjoy, that seems better than what is afforded to most."

"Diana," Juliana said quietly, "marriage doesn't have to immediately be about wild, passionate love. It can be about friendship. But it should be rooted in some measure of mutual affection if you are going to spend the rest of your life with the person. That is what pulled Edward and me together."

"You see?" Diana said, seizing on Juliana's words. "A marriage not based on love can work perfectly well."

"But Edward and I chose each other," Juliana continued gently. "We knew we suited in temperament and interests. What you're describing with Lord Ockham sounds more like… employment."

Marina opened her fan again. "Exactly. You speak of him as if he's hiring you to manage his estates, not courting you for a wife."

"And what's wrong with that?" Diana asked, though even as she spoke, she could hear how defensive she sounded. And she had a sudden urge to search for Lord Powis again. She wasn't even certain if she truly believed the things she said or if she had dug her heels into her plan. She struggled to move away from something once she set her mind on it.

"Oh, Diana." Hannah squeezed her arm. "You've always been far too stubborn for your own good."

Her closest friend knew her far too well. And she might be right. But it didn't change that she wanted to move her life forward. She didn't see Lord Powis, and she took that as a sign. The man was mesmerizing, but that didn't mean that there would be a future. He came from a line of libertine relatives, so it should come as no surprise that he was full of charm.

She was nothing if not practical, and Lord Ockham was practical. And she'd promised herself that she would take action this season. She was done waiting for her time to come.

Lord Ockham mentioned wanting fresh air, and perhaps… Perhaps this was an opportunity. If she could speak with him privately, away from the constraints of the ballroom, she might make her interest more clearly known.

"Ladies," she said, barely listening to their continued protests, "I find I'm quite warm. I think I'll step outside for some air."

"Diana—" Hannah began, recognizing the determined set of her friend's jaw. "I'm coming with you."

"No. Please. I'll only be a moment. And I need you to cover for me with Elias." Diana was already moving toward the terrace doors, before Hannah could refuse. For once in her carefully controlled life, she was going to take a risk. She was going to throw caution to the wind and see what might happen if she pursued what she wanted.

The cool evening air beckoned through the open doors, carrying with it the scent of early spring flowers. As she stepped onto the moonlit terrace, Diana felt a thrill of anticipation.

Diana descended the stairs of the terrace, searching the grounds for him. It was quiet and she didn't see anyone else. She moved deeper into the shadows of the garden, following the gravel path and expecting to come across Ockham at any moment.

She turned around in the maze and wasn't sure which way to

go. She heard other footsteps, and picked up her pace toward a turn in the path, hoping that she had caught up to him.

Rounding the corner of a hedge, she ran right into a hard, muscular frame.

Strong hands gripped her arms to steady her, and she looked up to find herself staring into the startled green eyes of Lord Powis. Her pulse raced as she realized how close they were standing. Close enough that she could feel his heart beat wildly against her chest. Close enough to catch the scent of sandalwood and something uniquely him.

"Lady Diana," he said more roughly than usual. "I... forgive me. I didn't expect anyone else to be out here."

I should step back, apologize, and return to the ballroom immediately. Instead, she found herself studying the strong line of his jaw, the way his dark hair had been slightly mussed by the evening breeze. Diana wanted to lose all control and allow her fingers to run her fingers through it.

"I was... that is, I came out for air." The words came out breathier than she intended.

His hands were still on her arms, warm even through the silk of her gloves. Neither of them moved to break the contact.

"As did I. The ballroom was rather overwhelming." His eyes scanned her face and the rest of her. "Are you quite all right? I didn't harm you when we collided, did I?"

Her pulse was racing, and she felt as though she couldn't quite catch her breath. But it had nothing to do with any injury and everything to do with the way he was looking at her with their bodies pressed together.

"I'm perfectly fine," she managed, though her voice betrayed her. "Just startled."

"Diana." The way he said her name, soft and wondering, made her stomach flutter.

Something shifted in his expression. His gaze dropped to her lips, and she found herself wondering what it would be like if he kissed her.

There was no space between them now. Or perhaps she had moved closer. She couldn't be sure.

"You should go back inside," he said quietly, but he made no move to release her. And he didn't sound as if he truly meant the words.

"Should I?" The words came out as barely more than a whisper.

His thumb traced across her arm where he held her. Such a small touch sent shivers through her entire body. "Yes. Before I do something we'll both regret."

But she didn't want to go back inside. She wanted to stay here in this garden with him, wanted to discover what would happen if she threw practicality to the wind, if she rose up on her toes, if she—

A crack of thunder split the air above them, so sudden and loud that Diana jumped. Almost immediately, the skies opened and rain began to pour down in earnest, soaking through her silk gown in seconds.

"Come." Graham took her hand without hesitation. "We must find shelter."

As they ran through the garden, her hand in his, Diana knew there would be no returning to practicality.

Whatever happened next would change everything. Because Diana realized the true danger wasn't the storm.

It was the man leading her through it.

CHAPTER THREE
Graham

GRAHAM'S PULSE HAMMERED as he gripped Diana's gloved hand, pulling her through the sudden downpour toward a white gazebo. Thunder crashed overhead, and her fingers tightened around his—a simple touch that sent warmth racing through him despite the cold rain soaking through his evening coat.

What the devil am I doing? Following her into the garden had been madness. He should have turned back the moment they'd entered the maze of shrubs and flowers. Being alone with her was far too dangerous. But watching her flee the ballroom, imagining her caught in this storm, had overridden every rational thought.

They reached the gazebo just as the rain turned violent, but not before they were both completely soaked. Graham released her hand only to place his palm against the small of her back, guiding her up the steps. Even through layers of silk and stays, the contact made him acutely far too aware of her.

"There," he panted, more breathless than their short run warranted. "We should be safe from the worst of it."

Diana turned to face him, and Graham's chest tightened. Rain had loosened wet golden locks that framed her face. Water droplets ran down her neck and then further, causing him to stare at her chest for just a bit too long. The sight of her was enough to make a man forget his own name.

"Thank you." She tucked a damp curl behind her ear. "Though I must say, this wasn't my intention for a garden stroll. I must look a dreadful fright."

"Dreadful?" Graham's voice came out rougher than intended. He couldn't look away from her. "You look…" Beautiful. Tempting. Like everything I never knew I wanted. "You look quite the opposite of dreadful."

Color rose in her cheeks despite the cool air. "You're very kind, my lord, but I'm hardly at my best as a drowned rat."

"Then I fear for the safety of every gentleman in London when you are at your best." The words escaped before he could stop them, and Graham felt his own face warm. "Forgive me. That was too forward."

Diana's eyes sparkled as she released a stream of giggles. "No forgiveness necessary. I rather enjoyed the compliment."

"I fear I'm terrible at all of this," Graham admitted, running a hand through his damp hair. "I'm still learning the art of polite conversation."

"You are much better than you believe yourself to be." Diana's voice was so soft and caring that he believed she meant it.

And then he noticed the way that she shivered.

"You're cold." Without thinking, Graham shrugged out of his evening coat, even though it was also soaked. He stepped closer to drape it around her shoulders. The gesture brought him within inches of her, close enough to see the way her lips parted slightly at his proximity.

"My lord?" Her soft whisper was almost lost in the thunder.

"Yes?" He let his hands linger on her shoulders where he'd settled his coat, unwilling to step away.

"I don't think I've ever met anyone quite like you." Her eyes searched his face, and he saw curiosity there, want, the same attraction that was consuming him. At least he preferred to believe it was there.

"Diana." He couldn't look away from her mouth, but he

could feel her in his grasp. "You're shivering again."

"Yet I don't believe I feel the cold."

His cock twitched at the suggestion in her tone. She was his every temptation and desire, and they were far too alone.

"This is dangerous," he murmured, but his hands were already moving to frame her face, his thumbs tracing the line of her cheekbones. He'd never even kissed someone before, but with her it felt like the most natural, right thing in the world to do.

"I know." Her hands came up to rest against his chest, and he wondered if she could feel the way his heart pounded. "But I find I don't much care at the moment."

The confession undid him completely. Graham lowered his head slowly, giving her every opportunity to pull away, to come to her senses, to remember all the reasons this was madness. Or perhaps to convince himself of the very same, but he feared that he was too far gone.

But instead, Diana rose up on her toes to close the distance between them.

Their lips met in a kiss that was nothing like he could have ever imagined. This was heat and need and wanting. When Diana's lips parted beneath his with a soft sigh, Graham felt everything else fade away.

She kissed him back with an eagerness that stunned him, her hands fisting in his waistcoat as if she needed something to anchor herself. He deepened the kiss, lost in the taste of her, the way she fit in his arms, and the soft sounds she made against his mouth.

His hands tangled in her damp hair, and he pressed her closer. Their tongues collided in something that overtook every single one of his senses. His cock was painful against the confines of his breeches. This was everything he'd been afraid to want—

"This is too perfect!" A sharp voice pierced the storm. "What have we here?"

Graham jerked back from Diana, his stomach dropping as Lady Theodosia and Lady Rebecca appeared at the gazebo entrance, their eyes bright with malicious delight as they took in the compromising scene. Matt had warned him about the vipers and their notoriety as the most vicious gossips of the *ton*.

Diana's hair was thoroughly mussed, her lips swollen from his kisses, and his coat draped around her shoulders. There was no hope of convincing the ladies that any intentions were honorable.

"Lady Diana," Lady Theodosia purred, her voice dripping with false concern. "I am certain your brother is going to have plenty to say about this."

Horror washed over Graham. In his selfish desire, he had done the unthinkable after he'd sworn he'd maintain control over himself that his father couldn't. And his first night in society and he has compromised an innocent woman. They both skirted a thin line toward scandal and ruin.

"Ladies," he said, moving protectively in front of Diana, though he knew it was far too late. "This isn't what it appears—"

"Oh, I think it's exactly what it appears," Lady Rebecca interrupted.

Graham watched Diana's face pale as the full implications hit her. Her family's reputation, her sisters' prospects, her own future—all hanging in the balance because of his weakness.

I'm exactly like my father after all, he thought bitterly.

But even as self-loathing flooded through him, Graham knew one thing with absolute clarity: he would do whatever was necessary to protect Diana from the consequences of his actions.

He had wanted to marry for love, and because his wife loved him in return.

Graham's chest burned with shame as he looked at a distraught Diana. Diana's wide eyes met his, with fear and confusion lingering there.

He knew what he must do to protect her, and that was far more important than how he had envisioned his future.

"You both can be the first to congratulate us," Graham said as calmly as he could. "Lady Diana had just accepted my marriage proposal."

Diana stiffened beside him. Her fingers trembled where they clutched his coat, and her lips parted as if she intended to speak, yet no words came. Her silence cut deep as the gravity of the situation set in.

Graham straightened his shoulders. Whether she wanted him or not, this lie had already become their truth.

They would marry.

CHAPTER FOUR
Diana

DIANA WASN'T CERTAIN she could believe what had just occurred. She blinked a few times, convinced that she was going to awaken from some insane dream. But she was still there, soaked beneath Lord Powis' coat with Lady Theodosia and Lady Rebecca far too filled with glee at the turn of events.

Diana understood immediately what the earl had done. Their betrothal was inevitable after how they'd been found. She'd been far too careless in believing they were actually alone and there weren't others caught in the storm. Being discovered alone in his arms embraced in a passionate kiss left them only two choices…marriage or ruination.

Marriage was the preferable option. But the weight of it brought tears to her eyes. Marriage was forever, and she hardly knew the man. He appeared kind and there was certainly attraction unlike what she even knew was possible.

That is what drove her to be so reckless and lose all of her practical sensibilities. But hadn't she set out into the garden to follow after a man? A man who wasn't the one she would now marry. One might argue her good sense had long vanished the moment she stepped foot into the dark.

She squared her shoulders and lifted her chin as she faced Theodosia. "I don't suppose you might let us share the news ourselves?"

"You know me better than that, Lady Diana," Theodosia replied. "I knew you were up to something the moment I saw you enter the garden."

"You followed me?"

"Indeed. Rebecca and I were taking the air when we noticed you slip away alone." Theodosia's smile was sharp as a blade. "And you certainly didn't disappoint."

Diana fisted her fingers tighter into Lord Powis's coat. She should have paid much better attention to her surroundings. Or better yet, she should have remained in the ballroom just as her friends had tried to convince her to do.

Theodosia reached her hand out and there were no rain droplets. The rain had stopped.

"Come, Rebecca," Theodosia said, linking arms with her companion. "We simply must share the news. This will be the talk of the season."

Diana watched as the two women hurried away without another word. By tomorrow, every drawing room in London would be buzzing with speculation about her hasty engagement.

"Diana," Graham said quietly, and she noticed he couldn't quite meet her eyes. "I'm sorry. I never intended—"

"You saved us both from complete ruin," she interrupted. "I should thank you."

"Don't." The word was sharp. "Don't thank me for compromising you."

The pain in his voice made her chest ache. He was blaming himself entirely, she realized. Taking on the full weight of their shared mistake.

She fought to find the words. Something that might offer comfort, but she wasn't certain what would comfort him. She didn't even know how to comfort herself.

"We should return," he said, offering his arm without looking at her. "I must speak with your brother."

As they walked back toward the ballroom, neither spoke a

single word. Her brother and father would be beside themselves. They'd plan a rushed wedding, if they didn't kill the earl first, and then she wasn't certain what her life would be. She didn't even know her betrothed's given name.

But underneath her fear, something else stirred. The memory of his arms around her, the way he'd looked at her before everything went horribly wrong. Perhaps there was something to build on, even if the foundation was shaky. Assuming he wanted that, too.

The ballroom erupted in whispers the moment they appeared. Diana felt every eye upon them, saw the way conversations stopped mid-sentence as they passed. The disheveled state of their appearances certainly didn't do them any favors.

She lifted her chin and smiled, refusing to give them the satisfaction of thinking they affected her. Even if she didn't wholly feel that way on the inside.

"Diana!" Hannah appeared at her elbow, face pale with concern. "Is what those vipers said true?"

"Lord Powis has asked for my hand," Diana said simply. There was no point in denying it when half the ballroom had already heard the news from Lady Theodosia.

Hannah's eyes widened. Behind her, Juliana, Tabitha, and Marina pushed through the crowd, their faces displaying various degrees of surprise and concern.

"But when—how—?" Tabitha stammered.

"That is a discussion for later," Diana whispered. "Now is not the time."

Her friends exchanged meaningful glances, clearly understanding that something significant had occurred. They formed a protective circle around her, their loyalty evident even as they took in her disheveled appearance and Powis's tense posture.

"Of course," Hannah said quickly, offering her a small, comforting smile.

Diana felt a rush of gratitude for their unwavering support.

Whatever questions they had would wait until they could speak privately.

Matt appeared at Powis's shoulder, and his expression also laced with concern.

"Graham," he said, his tone tight. "Congratulations on your betrothal to our Diana here."

At least Diana now knew the given name of her betrothed. That was a start. It didn't mean he would give her leave to refer to him as such, but it's a detail she should know about the man she was going to marry.

"Thank you," Graham replied stiffly, not meeting Matt's eye.

Before anyone could say more, Diana spotted Elias cutting through the crowd, much like a raging bull. She could see the way he strained to control his fury. And she drew a long breath to brace herself as curious onlookers watched the scene.

"Sister," Elias said when he reached them, his voice deadly calm. "I believe we need to speak."

"Elias," Diana began, but he held up a hand.

"Lord Powis," he started, barely hiding his contempt before he lowered his voice so only they could hear. "I believe I am owed the courtesy of a conversation."

Graham straightened, and to his credit he didn't cower at her brother's harsh tone. "Indeed, my lord."

"I'm pleased my sister accepted your proposal," Elias said loudly, so that his voice carried.

Diana saw several guests turn to listen, not bothering to hide their interest in the unfolding drama.

"As am I," Graham replied carefully.

Elias stepped closer, his smile never wavering for the benefit of their audience, but his voice dropped to a deadly whisper that only Diana and Graham could hear. "Though I find this rather suspicious. A man inherits a title and within hours of entering society has compromised an earl's daughter with a considerable dowry into marriage."

Diana felt the blood drain from her face at Elias's cruel words.

Graham went rigid beside her.

"Elias," Diana hissed.

But her brother wasn't finished. Still speaking quietly enough that only they could hear while maintaining his facade for the watching crowd. "I will see you on the dueling ground if you have a mind to take her dowry and abandon her in the country for mistresses and gambling halls."

Graham's jaw tightened, but he kept his voice equally low. "I am not of that mind, my lord. But I appreciate your concern."

Elias extended his hand to Graham for a formal shake. When Graham took it, Elias pulled him closer.

"Do you?" Elias asked, his nostrils flaring. "Because I do not make idle threats."

The threat hung in the air between them as the men faced each other, then released hands.

Graham nodded stiffly.

Elias straightened, extending his arm to his wife, Lydia, who had been watching the scene with concern. "Wonderful! We shall begin the wedding preparations tomorrow," he said loudly enough for nearby guests to hear. Then, dropping his voice once more, he continued, "And we'll continue our other conversation privately. Soon."

Lydia patted her husband's arm, urging him to maintain his composure.

"I must apologize for my brother," Diana whispered to Graham. "He shouldn't have—"

"He's right to do it," Graham cut her off quietly. "And I did compromise you."

Matt stepped closer to Graham's right. "Perhaps you should make the formal announcement," he suggested. "Put an end to the speculation."

"And then I'm taking my sister home," Elias added firmly.

Diana nodded just as Lady Fletcher approached with her husband in tow. "Lord Powis, Lady Diana, did we hear that an announcement may be in order?"

"You heard correctly," Graham said, not with a small smile that didn't reach his eyes.

"Oh, how wonderful!" Lady Fletcher exclaimed. "And at my ball. You are going to crush the matchmakers here tonight. They had their sights set on you, my lord."

Graham shifted uncomfortably on his feet, and Diana wished there was something she could say or do.

"Thank you," Diana managed, forcing a smile despite the turmoil in her chest.

"We'll make the announcement now," Lady Fletcher added. The woman would be talking about this for weeks to anyone who would listen.

"You're so very kind," Graham replied with what sounded like forced politeness.

Lord Fletcher called for attention and then Graham shared their news to the sea of guests. Diana stood beside him, watching the tittering and waving of fans as they were stared at and inspected. Both still soaked from their time in the rain.

She was almost grateful when Elias appeared to retrieve her from a line of people who had swarmed them to wish them well.

Graham and Matt followed as they took their leave, each party summoning their carriages and standing together in awkward silence.

Once the carriages rolled to a stop in front of the townhouse, Graham bowed formally to her before Elias could pull her away, remorse in expression. "Good night, Lady Diana. Lord Snowdon, Lady Snowdon." His eyes met Diana's again. "I shall call tomorrow."

"Good night, Lord Powis," Diana replied, the emotion of the events threatening to consume her.

She watched as Graham departed with Matt, before taking her brother's hand to step into her family's carriage. She seated herself across from Lydia and then Elias entered and sat beside his wife.

The moment the carriage door closed, even in the darkness

she could see the murderous expression he wore.

"What the devil happened in that garden?" Elias demanded.

"Elias," Lydia warned gently, placing a hand on his arm.

"No, my love. I want to hear from my sister what occurred." Elias raised his hand flippantly toward Diana. "Because either my sister lost her damned mind and willingly went off into the dark with a random man or the blackguard forced himself upon her. And I must know which."

Diana felt tears prick her eyes. "I was out in the garden and came across Lord Powis, and we were caught in the storm. We took shelter in the gazebo, and... Lady Theodosia and Lady Rebecca found us there."

"And why were you out in the garden alone and unchaperoned? When I noticed you were gone, I was told you were in the retiring room."

Diana's cheeks burned with shame. She could hardly tell him she'd been chasing after Lord Ockham and then ended up in the arms of a different man. "I needed air. The ballroom was stifling."

"Air," Elias repeated flatly. "So you decided to wander the grounds alone in the dark."

"What's done is done, Elias," Diana said, exasperated by her brother. "It just all happened so fast with the rain."

"Or the man saw an opportunity," Elias said harshly.

"You don't know that's what happened."

"I don't know much of anything about him. Or about what would possess you to allow the man to take certain liberties with you, if those horrid women speak the truth."

Lydia leaned forward and squeezed Diana's hand across the carriage. "What your brother means to say is that we just want to ensure that you are well after the events of the evening, dearest. This all happened so very quickly."

"I'm well aware," Diana fired back, harsher than she intended. "But neither of us planned for any of it. I know it."

"Time will tell," Elias huffed.

The carriage fell silent as they rolled through London's dark streets. Diana stared out the window, the weight of her brother's accusations settling over her like a shroud.

"You must at least like him if you entertained a kiss with the man?" Lydia asked gently.

"I do."

Elias practically growled beside her, but didn't say anything.

"What happens now?" Diana asked, though she wasn't certain she wanted to hear the answer. "How soon must we wed?"

"We shall discuss the marriage settlements with Powis," Elias said. "And we pray that whatever his motives, he proves to be a decent husband to you."

"And if he doesn't?"

Elias's expression grew even darker. "Then I'll make good on my promise to see him on the dueling ground."

As they turned onto their street, Diana felt the full impact of her precarious situation settle over her. In one reckless evening, she'd bound herself to a stranger whose motives, while she defended them, she couldn't be certain of. Her family's reputation hung in the balance, her sisters' futures were at stake, and she had no idea what kind of man she was truly marrying.

But she brought her fingers to her lips, remembering the heated kiss that got them into this mess. But as her world and future crumbled around her, all she could think about was when she would get to kiss him again.

CHAPTER FIVE

Graham

GRAHAM STARED AT the gossip column that his new secretary, Wilms, had left for him on his desk that morning. It wasn't hard to surmise that the post about "a certain new earl" and "a particular lady of impeccable breeding" discovered in "circumstances most compromising" at the Fletcher ball was about him and Diana.

He tossed the paper aside as just another reminder of how he'd failed them both. He had been weak. But the memory of Diana's rain-dampened dress clinging to her curves, the way her breath had hitched when he'd leaned closer, sent heat flooding right back through him as if it were occurring all over again.

He hadn't fully accepted it yet and probably wouldn't until he stood at the altar in a week's time and spoke his vows. If he could manage to keep his new brother-in-law from killing him before then. The meeting with Diana's brother just an hour ago had been a special kind of torture.

But he had allocated that Diana's entire dowry would be in her control. Thirty thousand pounds would certainly go a long way to help him out of his situation with Rothwell, but he wouldn't take from her to do it.

Even still, Elias was still hostile, to put it mildly. He wouldn't even allow Graham to see his betrothed until tomorrow.

If her brother was this incensed, he could only imagine how her father was going to react when he arrived in town.

He should feel terrible, and he did. But when he allowed himself a brief moment to think about what it would be like to be married to Diana, it made his pulse quicken in ways that had nothing to do with nerves. What would she look like on their wedding night, with her golden hair loose around her shoulders and her body bare before him?

If that is what she wished. If she had no interest in intimacy in their marriage. That would be torturous, but he'd honor her wishes. Besides he was being nothing more than a cad for thinking about such things when there were far more pressing matters.

His correspondence, for starters. He had to write to his mother and to John about this turn of events and he wasn't certain how to explain it without sounding like a complete fool. He'd just sent letters not a week ago informing them of the inheritance after he'd been hauled to London. And his mother might suffer apoplexy when she found out about his upcoming wedding. If he had the time to go speak with her directly, he would.

But he already had more on his plate than he knew how to manage, even with the secretary and valet that he employed with funds that needed to be saved to pay Rothwell. But a man could only handle so much on his own, and he needed to keep up appearances.

Graham moved to the writing desk in what had been his cousin's study, still unable to think of any of this as truly his. He pulled out a sheet of crisp parchment, letting his pen hover over the page for a long moment before he began.

Mother,

Please take a deep breath as you read this. I must share news that will come as quite the surprise, though I pray you will find it welcome. I am to be married within the week to Lady Diana

Armstrong, eldest daughter of the Earl of Snowdon.

I know this is sudden, and I regret that circumstances prevent me from explaining the situation in person. The attachment formed quite unexpectedly, but I expect you will be quite fond of my betrothed.

I understand your reluctance to travel to London, but I do hope you might reconsider attending the wedding.

Your devoted son,
Graham

He sealed the letter with more force than necessary, splattering the wax. The truth was far more complicated than he could commit to paper. How could he explain that he'd lost himself in a passionate kiss with a woman he'd just met, been caught in a compromising position, and was now bound to marry her? His mother would think he'd taken after his father.

Though perhaps he had. Because now that he'd kissed her once, he knew it would never be enough, and the desire he had for her was only growing. The taste of Diana's lips was all he could think about when he'd laid down to sleep last night.

Then there was the way she'd looked at him, as if she truly saw him rather than the title that never should have been his. The way her mind worked, quick and sharp. He found himself wondering what she thought about everything, what made her laugh, what books she preferred.

And then an idea came to him. Something that he knew would hold meaning to her. Something that he could do that might begin to make up for the situation he put them in.

He picked up his pen again and began his second letter.

John,

Hopefully you have the chance to read this before my mother, or I have little doubt she has already given you an earful on the matter.

I'm to be married to Lady Diana Armstrong within the week. I know this comes as a surprise, so please do your best to calm my mother.

This also means our arrangement regarding the horses must continue exactly as we discussed. I'll be establishing my household here in London for the immediate future while I sort through the demands of the title and a new bride.

I have one urgent request of you. Please send Luna to London immediately after you receive this. Have her brought by our most trusted groom, as she'll be a gift for my bride.

You will do well to continue on with the business.

Your cousin,
Graham

Graham rang for his butler, Mitchell. "Have these dispatched immediately by messenger. They must reach their destination today."

"Of course, my lord." The man took the missives and departed, closing the door behind him.

Only a few moments had passed before there was a knock at the door again.

"Come," he called, and Mitchell appeared just inside the door again.

"A gentleman to see you, my lord. Mr. Silas Rothwell."

Graham's chest tightened. He'd been dreading this visit, but hoped the man might take a bit more time. But from the letters he'd already received, he could tell that patience wasn't the man's strong suit. "Show him to the morning room. I'll be along shortly."

When the butler departed, Graham allowed himself exactly thirty seconds to panic. His pulse raced as he considered what he would even say. Forty-five thousand pounds. His dissolute cousin hadn't left any funds available. Only properties, a couple of which were already mortgaged. He needed more time to sort through it all and determine what he would do.

He straightened his shoulders and made his way to face the blackguard his cousin ran up gambling debts with. The man who had become Graham's problem he didn't want nor ask for.

Rothwell stood with his back to the door, examining a landscape painting. He was younger than Graham had expected, perhaps in his thirties, with a silver streak in his hair and the slimy look of someone who'd never done honest work.

"Lord Powis," Rothwell said without turning. "How delightful of you to receive me."

"Mr. Rothwell." Graham kept his voice level. "To what do I owe the pleasure?"

"Oh, I think we both know why I'm here." The man finally faced him, his pale eyes riddled with amusement. "I trust you've had time to prepare my funds given the notes I hold?"

"I'm still reviewing the estate records. These matters take time—"

"Time?" Rothwell scoffed. "My lord, your cousin's debts have been accruing interest for months. So I have reached the end of my generosity. And I am out of time to wait."

Sweat gathered at the base of Graham's neck. "I understand the urgency. However, liquidating assets of this magnitude requires careful consideration—"

"I don't care how you get my money." Rothwell cut him off as he moved closer. "I wonder, does your charming betrothed know your situation? Lady Diana, isn't it? You've done well for yourself to be sure. And quickly, too. I'm sure her dowry will be a nice start to paying me what I'm owed."

The threat struck him. Graham's hands clenched at his sides, willing himself not to plant the man a deserved facer. "Stay away from her. She is hardly your concern."

"On the contrary. Until I have my funds, everything is my concern." Rothwell smiled, showing too many teeth. "But I'm a reasonable man. Shall we say… three weeks? That should give you sufficient time to arrange matters."

Three weeks. His wedding was in a matter of days, and then he'd have to quickly do what he could to raise the funds and expedite the sale of his chosen properties. "And if I cannot—"

"Oh, but you will." Rothwell adjusted his gloves with deliberate care. "Because the alternative would be most unfortunate for your new family. The Earl of Snowdon has such a sterling reputation, even if his son used to be a frequent patron at the tables before he went and fell in love. It would be tragic if you were the one to bring that perfect family to their knees before the *ton*... and your pretty little wife left as nothing but a cast out widow."

Graham's vision blurred with fury. "Keep your threats directed at me and leave my betrothed and her family out of this."

"Then I shall expect my funds." Rothwell moved toward the door, pausing at the threshold. "Three weeks and not a day longer, my lord. I do hope you won't disappoint me."

And with that, the man was gone, leaving Graham to contemplate what he must do next.

He wasn't even certain if he could close a sale on a single property in that amount of time. And likely not at a loss.

His hands shook as he reached for the crystal decanter on the side table and poured himself a generous measure of brandy. The liquid burned his throat, but it helped steady his nerves enough to think clearly.

He returned to his study on unsteady legs and collapsed into the chair behind the desk. Graham buried his face in his hands. He should call off the engagement. If it wouldn't ruin her and her entire family, he would. But it was far too late for that.

He would find a way out of this mess and ensure she never had cause to worry. He had to.

There was little he could do until the details of his holdings were made available to him. He needed a distraction from the mounting anxiety of the walls of his circumstances closing in on him. Graham stood and wandered to the bookshelves lining the study, hoping to find something—anything—to take his thoughts off his impossible situation.

The previous earl had quite the collection of books. Given the amount of dust that had collected on some of the titles, he could assume they weren't purchased by his predecessor.

He ran his fingers along the spines of the books as he read each of them. He looked for texts on agriculture that might help prepare him for the estates he'd now have to oversee the management of.

Wedged between a tome on Roman history and a book of sermons, his fingers stopped on an interesting spine. The leather binding was newer than the rest, unmarked by any title. Graham pulled it free and opened it to the first page, expecting perhaps a journal or collection of papers.

What he found instead made his face burn.

Pleasures of the Body proclaimed the title page in elegant script. He continued to the next page and was met with a drawing of a man on top of a woman. He couldn't help but study the page, then turned to the next and the man and woman were in a different position, with her sitting on top of the man. It was drawn from behind the woman with her up on her knees, so it was clear where the man's cock was meant to enter.

He snapped the book shut, his pulse racing with all of the blood seemingly running straight to his cock.

Graham glanced toward the door, ensuring he was truly alone, then unable to stop his curiosity, he opened the book again. The illustrations were… detailed. Very detailed. Warmth continued to spread through his body as he turned the pages, finding diagrams and explanations that made him respond in ways that were enlightening, and reminded him of his inexperience.

He had been a virgin by choice, set on not being the man his father was and marrying for love. And all of that was going to change in a few days if his wife would have him. And pleasing his new bride caused him nearly as much anxiety as settling the business with Rothwell.

The thought of disappointing Diana on their wedding night, of revealing just how inexperienced he truly was, was more than he could bear. The least he could do was ensure that he satisfied her in the physical aspects of their marriage.

He closed the book and tossed it onto his desk. He was a grown man, reduced to learning about such things from a text. But he supposed he'd rather have the knowledge in the text than to enter the marriage bed with only what he had overheard from boisterous, bragging men in pubs.

A soft knock sounded in the room. "Come," he called, and then winced at the unfortunate double meaning.

Matt entered, looking insufferably cheerful given the circumstances. "Good morning! I told Mitchell that I'd see myself to your study. You look like hell."

"Your powers of observation remain sharp as ever." Graham gestured to a chair, relieved that the ache between his legs had dissipated.

Matt settled himself with the easy grace that came from being born to his position. "The gossip rags are having a field day. Half the *ton* is calling it terribly romantic, while the other half suspects the covering of a scandal."

"And which half are you?"

"Neither. I'm a friend to you both, and I know your character enough to know that you didn't do anything overly untoward. Even if it wasn't well done of you." Matt's expression grew somber. "Though you are going to have a hell of time convincing Elias of the same."

"I'm well aware," he replied. Elias said as much multiple times. "He's the least of my worries."

Matt's eyes widened. "And what do you mean by that?"

Graham cursed himself silently. He hadn't meant to let that slip. Given the way Matt was studying him, he wouldn't let it drop either. There was no taking it back now.

"Graham?" Matt's voice held more concern. "What's going on?"

For a moment, Graham considered deflecting, making some excuse about wedding nerves or family pressures. But the weight of carrying this burden alone was crushing him, and he knew that he could trust Matt.

"My cousin didn't just leave me a title and estates," Graham said finally, his voice barely above a whisper. "He left me his debts as well. Gambling debts. Forty-five thousand pounds worth."

The color drained from Matt's face. "Christ, Graham. That's—"

"A fortune, yes. And the man left nothing in his coffers." Graham quickly reached for the decanter of brandy and a couple of glasses. "And before you ask, I will not use Diana's dowry to resolve this matter. I won't start our marriage by stealing what should be hers to settle my arse of a cousin's dealings."

He poured them each a glass of the amber liquid.

"But surely there must be some way to raise the funds. The unentailed properties—"

"My solicitor is gathering complete reports on everything. Once I know what I have to work with, I'll decide what can be sold." Graham met Matt's eyes. "I wanted to keep this to myself, but... well, now you know. And I don't want anyone else to know about this."

Matt was quiet for a minute, then took a long sip of the glass that Graham pushed into his hand. "How long do you have?"

"Three weeks. Rothwell made that quite clear this morning when he paid me a visit."

"Rothwell?" Matt's jaw tightened dangerously. "That snake was here? Graham, you must use caution in dealing with that man."

"I'm aware of his reputation." Graham's voice was grim. "But I have little choice in the matter. He's made it clear that if I don't pay, Diana and her family will suffer for it."

"That bastard threatened Diana?" Matt was on his feet now, pacing. "Graham, there has to be something we can do. I could—"

"No." Graham's voice was firm. "I won't drag you into this mess. I just... I needed someone to know the truth. Someone who could vouch for my character if things go badly."

Matt stopped pacing and fixed him with a stare. "You think I'd abandon you in this?"

"I think you're a good friend, but this isn't your burden to bear."

"Like hell it isn't." Matt sat back down, leaning forward intensely. "You're about to marry into one of my closest friend's families. Diana is like a sister to me. If you think I'm going to stand by and watch Rothwell destroy both of you—"

"Matt, I don't intend to let it come to that. I will find a proper way out of this and then it will be done."

Matt pushed his glass to Graham, indicating he wanted another pour. "You're a good man, Graham. A better man than most would be in your situation. And Diana... she's going to need to know the truth."

"I know." Graham ran his hand through his hair. "But not yet. Just let me solve this so she needn't worry. I don't want to put that on her."

Matt nodded slowly. "Fair enough. But promise me this—if you need help, if there's anything I can do, you'll ask."

"I promise."

Graham filled each of their glasses again and they downed them in silence.

But even as the brandy burned in his chest, Graham knew one truth he could not escape—if he failed, it would not be only his ruin, but Diana's too.

CHAPTER SIX
Diana

DIANA SMOOTHED HER pale yellow morning dress over her lap, forcing herself to keep from fidgeting in her seat. Lord Powis—Graham—would be calling within the hour. It was the first time she'd see him since two nights ago when they'd ended up betrothed.

She popped up from the settee and moved about the room. She'd barely slept since it happened, her mind churning over the events in the gazebo. The memory of his hands settling his coat around her shoulders, the way his voice had roughened just before she had pressed her lips so his. The memory did things to her that she could never speak to anyone.

"Diana, you're pacing again." Lydia's voice carried gentle amusement from her seat by the drawing room window. "It's not going to make him appear any sooner. Besides, all will be well."

Diana paused mid-step and turned to face her sister-in-law, who was working on her embroidery by the window. "Easy for you to say. You didn't have to endure Elias's lecture about maintaining propriety with my 'fortune-hunting betrothed.'"

"You know your brother." Lydia's needle paused. "Let's hope your father has a more reasonable head."

Diana's stomach twisted again. Papa. She could already picture the look of disappointment on his face.

Before Diana could respond, Mitchell appeared in the doorway. "Lord Powis has arrived, my lady."

Diana's stomach dropped to her slippers. "Show him in, please."

She took a steadying breath, then another, but it did little to settle her nerves. When Graham appeared in the doorway, her breath caught completely.

He looked different in the afternoon light. Certainly no less handsome, perhaps even more so. His chestnut hair was perfectly arranged and his form nicely filled out the cut of his fine clothing. But when their eyes met, she caught a flash of the same nervous energy she felt herself.

"Lady Diana." He bowed precisely. "Lady Snowdon. Thank you for receiving me."

"Lord Powis," Diana curtsied, which felt odd to do for her intended. "Please, do sit. Tea?"

"That would be most welcome." He took the chair across from hers, close enough that she could detect his sandalwood scent.

Lydia remained in her seat across the room by the window, while Diana took to pouring for her and Graham. After she handed him his cup, she picked up her own and stared at it, searching for something intelligent to say. The silence stretched just long enough to become noticeable when Graham cleared his throat.

"I do hope you are faring well after all that has occurred." His eyes held genuine concern.

"Indeed. Though I fear my poor maid nearly swooned when she saw my dress." Diana found herself smiling at the memory. She might keep that dress forever.

Graham's mouth twitched with suppressed amusement. "I don't see any lemon cakes on your tray. I suppose we bypassed the need for them."

Diana laughed despite herself. "Yes, it appears that they are wholly unnecessary. But if you are feeling slighted, I can ensure

Cook prepares some for you."

"I quite like lemon." And when he flashed her a full grin, he almost made her heart stop.

There was something about him that instantly pulled her in. She felt it that night, and it was still alive and well in her drawing room. But that was dangerous. She didn't know anything about him, nor what he believed the marriage would be.

She set down her teacup, suddenly serious. "Forgive me for speaking directly, I supposed you find out now that it is my usual course, but I know so little about you. And if we're to be married…"

"You'd like to know who you're binding yourself to," Graham finished. "I understand completely. I feel the same."

"So tell me what I should know about you, then?"

He appeared to contemplate her question. "My given name is Graham Clive, which I give you leave to always use. I owned a business breeding horses before I inherited the title that was in my father's family for generations. My personal mount is Midnight, and I have him here with me in London." He fixed his gaze with hers and then leaned closer as if he were going to tell her a secret. "I quite like the color blue, enjoy reading, and detest artichokes."

Diana stifled a giggle. "That is all quite helpful information."

"Your turn," he said, sipping his tea and then setting the saucer to the side.

She tucked a loose curl behind her ear. "Well, I ran our household from around age twelve until last year when Elias married Lydia."

Diana glanced over to make sure Lydia hadn't heard her as she didn't wish to offend her, then continued. "You've met Elias, but I also have two younger sisters, Jenny and Grace. I can't think of a food I don't like, my favorite color is pink, and I also like to read. Mostly texts on agriculture, livestock, and estate planning. I like to be useful, so I began learning so that I might help Papa…or my future husband."

Graham focused intently on her the entire time, as though he truly cared about everything she had to say.

He appeared to ponder her words for a moment and then leaned forward. "I am expecting information on my estates and holdings in a few days. Perhaps you might like to give them a look and give me your assessment."

She clasped her hands together at her chest. "Do you mean it?"

"Of course. I'd appreciate your input."

It was almost too good to be true. It wasn't common for a man of their society to ask a woman for help or input. But it was just the kind of partnership she had wanted with a husband. Her practical match that she was so hellbent on before her entire world shifted.

Suddenly, all she could think about was how entranced she'd been with him. And as much as she didn't want to judge him by his relations, but given their situation, she couldn't help but wonder if he might honor their marriage vows. And she had to know.

"Once we are married, do you intend that we will lead separate lives?"

It was the most proper way she could think to ask what she really wanted to know.

His face contorted to a deep frown. "Is that what you want?"

"No," she said quickly, before she could stop herself.

"Good," he replied, releasing a long breath as if he were relieved, which put her more at ease.

"It sounds like we are starting things as well as we can," she said, trying to alleviate the awkwardness. "I suppose that is better than most marriages. We might even spend a bit of time together."

Graham opened his mouth to say something and then closed it again.

"What? Tell me what you were going to say."

He remained quiet for a moment, then glanced over at Lydia

and then lowered his voice. "I thought perhaps after we're married, I might teach you to ride a horse. We could spend time together that way, if you'd like."

Diana's breath caught. "You would really teach me?"

"If you want to learn. I know your father forbade it, but as my wife..." His voice trailed off, but she understood his meaning.

"I would love that more than anything." Diana leaned forward eagerly and lowered her voice to a whisper. "But why wait until after we're married? We could start now, couldn't we?"

Graham shifted uncomfortably. "Well, your brother hates me enough as it is, and your father is likely to feel the same. They would never allow you to come to my home for riding lessons."

"They don't need to know."

Graham looked torn. "Your brother will have my head if he finds out."

Diana glanced quickly at Lydia to see that she was still intently focused on her embroidery, then back at Graham. "I don't want to wait. I've dreamed of this for years. Can I even just meet your horse?" She looked up at him through her lashes. "Please, Graham."

It was the first time she'd referred to him in such an intimate way, and it appeared to have the desired effect. And she watched his resolve crumble.

"Fine. But we will only start with the basics until after we are married."

"Take your leave now, and I shall walk you out," Diana chirped, practically bouncing with excitement.

Graham just shook his head at her and then rose from his seat. "I've enjoyed our time together, my lady. We shall do this again soon."

Diana tried not to giggle at his stiff exchange.

"Good day, Lady Snowdon," he called over to Lydia.

She looked up and nodded at him.

"I'll walk you out," Diana said, rising from her seat. Lydia wouldn't follow if she just walked him to the door.

Diana took his arm and as soon as they were in the hall, she leaned close to him. It reminded her far too much of their kiss and made her wish that he would kiss her again. She got so entranced with the notion that she almost forgot the purpose for his hasty departure.

"Your townhouse is only a couple blocks from here," she started. I'll sneak out and meet you at your mews."

He came to a dead stop. "You shall do no such thing."

His reaction confused her as she thought they had just agreed to the lessons.

"Meet me behind your house in fifteen minutes and I'll escort you. I'm not going to have my betrothed putting herself in danger."

It warmed her heart that he cared so much for her safety. And that he would give her one of the things that she'd always wanted most. The freedom to ride.

"Very well. Fifteen minutes. I'll be there."

He cast her a concerned look as if he might go back on the plan, but then continued forward. "I'll be waiting."

She nodded excitedly and then released his arm so that he could depart. Then she turned on her heel and went back to the drawing room.

"Did you have a nice time?" Lydia asked, eyeing her curiously.

"I did." And she meant that. "I think we might suit well."

Very well, in fact. It might not have been a love match or happened how her family might have liked, but the thought of marrying Graham Clive in less than a week didn't fill her with dread. And she was taking that as a positive. Besides, it's not like she had any choice anyway, so she might as well make the most of it.

"I think I'll go to my chamber and read for a while. All this has been rather overwhelming and we still have more preparations ahead."

"Of course, dearest. Rest will do you good."

Diana made her way upstairs, but instead of going to her room, she slipped down the servants' stairs and out through the kitchen. Her stomach was in knots as she made her way to the alley behind her house.

What am I doing? This is madness. If she were to be caught, she would never hear the end of it and it would only make things more awkward with her family. But as soon as she reached the alley and saw Graham waiting there, all her doubts disappeared.

"Are you certain about this?" he asked as soon as she approached.

"Absolutely."

Graham took her hand and looked in both directions then led her through the alleys so they stayed off of the main streets. It was very likely that someone might see them, but since they were already betrothed, there wasn't much else that could be done to them.

Once they finally reached Graham's mews, he released her hand. "Wait here."

He went inside and a few moments later he came out walking alongside a huge black horse. She didn't know much about horses, but this one was massive and positively gorgeous in the way his coat shined in the sunlight.

Diana approached slowly, eyeing the horse. "Is this...?"

"Midnight. He's very gentle." Graham held the horse's lead rope. "Would you like to meet him properly?"

Diana nodded, suddenly nervous. Graham took her hand and guided it to the horse's neck.

"Just stroke him gently. Like that."

The horse's coat was warm and soft under her palm. "He's beautiful. Hello there, Midnight."

"Would you like to try sitting on him?"

Diana's eyes widened. "Now?"

"Just for a moment. So you can see how it feels."

Before she could lose her nerve, she nodded. Graham led Midnight to a nearby mounting block.

"I'll help you up," he said, positioning himself behind her. "And I won't let you go."

His hands settled on her waist, and even through her stays she could feel their warmth. Her breath caught as his thumbs brushed just below her ribs. When he lifted her as if she weighed nothing, his body pressed briefly against hers, leaving her breathless.

Sitting sideways on Midnight's back, Diana felt a rush of exhilaration. "I'm actually on a horse."

Graham was standing close, one hand resting on her knee to steady her and the other on her hip while he remained standing on the mounting block. The contact made every part of her body aware of his presence.

"How does it feel?"

"Like flying." She looked down at him, acutely aware of his hand on her leg. "Like freedom."

His gaze intensified, and he tightened his grip on her hip slightly. They didn't break eye contact as he released her leg to grab her other hip and lift her down, and her body slid against his. She felt that familiar beat of his heart when her feet landed on the mounting block.

"Thank you," she whispered.

Graham lowered his head slightly and she held her breath waiting for the moment that his lips touched hers. She wrapped her arms around his neck to encourage him.

"His butler said he may be back here."

They both heard the voice and Graham jerked his chin toward the sound.

"He hadn't returned home since he called on Diana."

Diana's blood ran cold. *Elias.* How had he known she was there? And who was he speaking to?

Graham cursed under his breath and motioned for her to step inside the building. "Stay here," he whispered. "Don't make a sound."

As footsteps approached, Diana pressed herself against the

wall, trying to steady her uneven breaths hoping that her brother hadn't seen her.

"So this is the man?" another voice said outside of the stables.

Diana covered her mouth to keep from gasping.

Her father was on the other side of the wall.

CHAPTER SEVEN

Graham

GRAHAM STEPPED OUT from where he'd hidden Diana just as he could hear footsteps and voices moving closer. It would seem that Elias wasn't alone, and it wasn't out of the realm of possibility that the man hadn't ruled out the notion of challenging him to a duel.

"Lord Powis," Elias called as he rounded the corner. Behind him walked a tall, distinguished man with graying hair and deep dimples even with the scowl he wore. The resemblance was unmistakable.

Graham straightened his shoulders and stepped forward. "You must be Lord Snowdon. Viscount." He bowed formally, his pulse stuttering wildly. "I wasn't expecting—"

"I just arrived," the Earl of Snowdon cut him off. His tone was firm, but there was also a kindness in his eyes. "I thought it best not to delay meeting the man who will marry my daughter."

"I am glad you have arrived safely." Graham prayed Diana had the sense to stay hidden. "Perhaps we might continue this conversation somewhere more comfortable? I could offer you some refreshment at the house."

"This location suits me fine," the earl said curtly. "I prefer to speak plainly, Lord Powis. My son has explained the matter to me, and it would seem that we have no choice but to go along with this little arrangement. But you should know that if my daughter is treated in any way that I don't deem acceptable, I will not hesitate to bring her home. I don't give a damn what the law says. Do I make myself clear?"

Graham's spine went rigid. "I can assure you, my lord, that your daughter can do as she wishes in our marriage."

"That's not what I asked." The earl stepped closer. Suddenly his eyes weren't quite so kind anymore. "I asked if I made myself clear? I will not tolerate any mistreatment of Diana. She may be forced into this marriage, but she deserves happiness and comfort nonetheless."

A thud came from just inside the stables where Diana was. The men noticed and glanced toward the opening. Graham forced himself not to glance in that direction and took a side step to further block the entrance.

"You are clear, my lord," Graham said firmly, recapturing their attention. "And I intend to see that she is content."

The earl studied him for a moment. "Good. Because despite the circumstances that brought you together, I expect this marriage to be a real one. Diana deserves a husband who remains faithful and doesn't make a fool of her with other women and gambling."

"If you knew me at all, you'd know that shall never be a concern," Graham said, meaning every word.

Something in the earl's expression softened slightly. "You give me the correct responses." His voice grew harder again. "The problem is that we don't know you. So I have no choice but to take you at your word."

"You have nothing to worry about. I assure you that I mean what I say." This was all the more reason that no one could know about his financial matters. Her family would never believe that what had occurred to result in this marriage was purely an accident.

The earl nodded curtly. "Then we understand each other." He turned to Elias. "Come. We should return home. I'd like to speak to Diana next."

Graham's stomach clenched at the mention of Diana's name, but he kept his expression neutral. "Thank you for taking the time to meet with me, my lord. I look forward to us getting to know each other better."

"As do I." The earl's expression was unreadable. "Good day, Lord Powis."

Graham bowed as the two men departed, waiting until their footsteps faded completely before he sagged against the wall of the mews and released a deep breath. Diana's father was clearly a man who loved his daughter fiercely, and Graham had no doubt the earl would follow through on his threats if given cause. The earl and his son wouldn't think twice about ripping him limb from limb.

Diana appeared in the doorway. "Are they gone?" she hissed.

"Yes," Graham said, kicking off the wall and standing at the entry. "Though I'm not certain I will ever win over your father or brother."

"What did you mean when you said that if my father knew you at all that other women and gambling wouldn't be a concern?"

Graham felt heat rise in his cheeks. He forgot that she would have heard the entire conversation. And he didn't exactly wish to confess that he was completely inexperienced. He wasn't even certain she'd believe him anyway. But he had to give her something. Something real. "I watched my mother suffer because of my father's... appetites. I swore I would never put a woman through that."

Diana's expression softened. "Your father was unfaithful?"

"Among other things." Graham's jaw tightened, then he shook off the thoughts of his father. "And I detest gambling, almost as much as artichokes."

Diana's lips curled into the most adorable grin. "And I've learned a few more things about you."

"I'm afraid that is all the education we have time for at present. Your father is on his way home to speak with you."

Her face shifted to an expression of panic. "How am I to get home without being caught?"

"We will take the alleys as quickly as we can so you can sneak back into your house. Or at least get to the garden."

He took her hand and they slipped out of the mews and through back streets, Graham keeping watch for anyone as they crossed each short block.

At the corner of her street, Graham stopped. "I'll keep watch until you're safely inside."

Diana turned to face him, and for a moment they simply looked at each other.

"Graham," she said softly. "Thank you for being honest with me about your father. Honesty is important in a marriage."

The guilt of the situation he was hiding from her gnawed at him, but he told himself he was doing what was best. To give them the best chance. Their marriage wouldn't start with love, but there was attraction and connection. And he couldn't ruin that before they'd even started.

He couldn't speak, so he just nodded.

She rose on her toes and brushed a kiss to his cheek, lingering just a moment longer than before.

"Thank you for today. I hope to see you tomorrow," she whispered, then turned and walked swiftly toward her house.

Graham watched until she disappeared inside, his hand rising unconsciously to touch the spot where her lips had touched his skin. He was doing the right thing. The attraction and quick comfort between them couldn't be coincidence. He did mean every word he said to her father. Somehow she had quickly become the person that would matter the most to him over anyone else.

Once he resolved the one matter hanging over his head, there was a change that their marriage might actually become something real. Because Diana Armstrong would be easy to love.

THE NEXT MORNING, Graham was up early, as was his habit from his years of running a business. After breaking his fast, he was informed that Luna had arrived with one of his grooms, Thomas. They must have traveled some through the night to get her here.

After Graham questioned the man about the happenings back at his old home, he sent Thomas to settle the horse in the stables with the other horses. Then Graham immediately ventured to his study to review the letters that Thomas had brought with him.

First was a letter from John.

Graham,

I read your letter three times before I believed the words. Marriage so soon? I hardly know what to think, but congratulations are certainly in order.

Fair warning your mother is… well, I'll let her tell you herself. But you might want to prepare for quite the lecture when you see her next.

I look forward to meeting your new bride. And don't worry about things here, as I have everything well in hand.

Your cousin,
John

He immediately rang for Mitchell and then set John's letter aside and picked up his mother's, bracing himself for her reaction.

My dearest son,

What in heaven's name have you done?

Marriage? And within a week of inheriting that dratted title? Have you taken complete leave of your senses?

I am, of course, delighted that you've found someone to share your life with. But darling boy, this haste concerns me deeply. I expect you to tell me everything when I see you.

I shall make arrangements to travel to London. I have

commitments here and I am not certain I will be there in time for the wedding, but should arrive within a fortnight. Please forgive me for missing the ceremony, but I'd be out of place in a grand London event.

All my love,
Mother

Graham set the letter down and pushed aside the disappointment that his own mother wouldn't be there for the wedding. But at least she was coming to London. That was at least something. He knew how it felt to be cast into a society you weren't even certain you wanted to be a part of. And doing so was his burden, not hers.

He pulled a clean piece of parchment to begin a reply. As soon as he dipped his pen in ink, his study door flew open and then clicked closed.

And Diana stood leaning against the door.

"Diana." Graham shot to his feet, nearly knocking over his inkwell in the process. "What are you doing here? How did you—"

"I know my way around a townhouse," Diana said with a mischievous smile. "I just got lucky when I assumed you were in your study."

Graham raked his fingers through his hair. "You shouldn't have snuck out without an escort. Anything could have happened." Even as he said it, he couldn't help but drink in the sight of her. She was wearing a deep blue walking dress that brought out her eyes, and her cheeks were pink from the morning air.

"I just couldn't wait any longer," she said, pushing off from the door and moving further into his study. "I wanted another riding lesson."

His mind went to an impure place from her words. And it had everything to do with a certain book that he'd spent all of last night examining. He drew a deep breath, doing his best to push that particular mental image aside.

"It's far too dangerous with your father in town now, too.

We shall be married soon enough and we can continue our lessons then."

Diana waved a dismissive hand. "Elias dragged Papa to their club with Hudson. They shall never know I'm gone." Her eyes sparkled with mischief. "Besides, you already agreed."

Graham stared at her, realizing that there was likely never a single time in their lives that he would be able to tell her no to anything. "You're going to be the death of me, aren't you?"

"I certainly hope not," Diana said with a grin. "That would make for a very short marriage indeed."

Despite himself, Graham found his lips twitching with suppressed laughter. "You're completely mad."

"Perhaps. But I'm also determined to learn to ride." She stepped closer still, close enough that he could see the gold flecks in her blue eyes. "Please, Graham? Just a short lesson?"

There was absolutely no way he would ever be able to deny this woman anything.

"A short lesson," he said finally. "And then I take you straight home."

Diana clapped her hands together in delight. "Thank you!"

Graham just shook his head, questioning his sanity for allowing himself to be talked into a situation that would only make her father hate him more. "Come then. I actually have a surprise for you."

"What sort of surprise?" Diana asked, practically bouncing on her toes.

"You'll see." Graham couldn't help but smile at her enthusiasm. He would give her anything she wanted if it kept her smiling at him the way she was.

They made their way to the stables, taking care to avoid anyone in Graham's household seeing him. With Diana's hand in his, and her body pressed close to his when they paused before darting around corners, he became far too aware of her. The memory of that damned book's illustrations kept flashing through his mind, making him sensitive to every gentle touch.

When they reached the stables, they found Luna settled into a stall. The mare's ears pricked forward at their approach, and she nickered softly.

"Oh," Diana breathed, rushing to the stall. "This is a beautiful horse."

That she was. She was solid black, almost identical to Midnight, but just a bit smaller.

"She's yours," Graham said, running his fingers along the horse's neck. "I thought she would make a good wedding present. And I trained her myself."

Diana's eyes widened. "Mine? Truly?" She beamed at him, and the joy on her face made his chest tighten. "Graham, I... I don't know what to say."

"You don't need to say anything." He moved closer, watching as Diana tentatively reached out to stroke Luna's nose. "She's gentle as a lamb but still quite spirited. Perfect temperament for a lady's mount."

"She's absolutely perfect." Diana's voice was soft with wonder. "What's her name?"

"Luna. She was born on the night of a full moon." Graham smiled at the memory. "I thought the name suited her."

Diana turned to face him fully, and there were tears in her eyes. "No one has ever given me anything so wonderful."

The raw emotion in her voice made Graham's heart do a little flip in his chest. Without thinking, he reached out to cup her face gently. "You deserve this, Diana. You deserve everything."

For a moment, they simply looked at each other, the air between them charged. Something that felt dangerously close to losing control again.

"Thank you," she whispered with watery eyes.

Graham brushed his thumb across her cheek, catching a tear. "You are indeed quite welcome."

"Can we still have my lesson?"

Graham nodded, trying again to stop his thoughts from going to a place they shouldn't. "Let's get her saddled."

Within minutes, Luna had been saddled by the groom that was nearby, who had insisted on taking over when Graham tried to saddle her himself. But he sent the servants away afterward since the fewer who knew about their lessons, the better.

"Ready?" Graham asked.

Diana nodded eagerly.

He gripped her hips and set Diana in the seat. "Up you go."

Diana settled into the sidesaddle with growing confidence, and Graham adjusted her stirrups. When he looked up to check her position, she appeared to be the happiest woman in all of London.

"How does that feel?"

"Perfect," Diana said softly, her eyes meeting his. "Everything about this feels perfect. I love her."

Graham's hands lingered on her leg longer than necessary, and he saw Diana's breath catch. And she didn't look away from him.

"We should begin," he said, though he didn't move away.

"Yes," Diana whispered, but she was looking at his lips now, and Graham felt his control slipping.

He forced himself to step back. "Let's start with some simple movements."

Diana guided Luna with Graham's instruction. She improved each time she did so, and became more confident in the saddle.

"Excellent," he said as she completed another circle in the alley and returned to the mews. "You're a natural. Although I do believe we are going to have to get you a proper riding habit."

"Thank you." Diana beamed. "I've never had a riding habit before."

He took the reins and tied them to a wooden beam. "Here, let me help you down."

Her hands came to rest on his shoulders as he reached up to help her from the saddle. But instead of setting her down quickly, he lifted her down slowly, her body sliding against his until she was standing pressed against him.

She wrapped her arms around his neck, pulling him even closer.

"We shouldn't," he breathed, even though he made no effort to back away.

"I know," she whispered back, but she also did not attempt to move. "But I must thank you properly."

"Diana—"

She silenced him by pressing her lips to his, and Graham was lost. His hands tangled in her hair as she kissed him with a sweetness that quickly turned desperate. When she made a soft moan of pleasure against his mouth, he just about came completely undone.

Her hands moved from his shoulders to his chest, and he groaned against her mouth. Every touch, every soft sigh she made, wound him tighter. This was dangerous, this overwhelming need that threatened to consume every shred of his control.

But Diana was pressing closer, and he knew he was already lost. His lips moved to her throat, tasting the salt of her skin, and she arched against him with a gasp.

"Diana," he managed, his only attempt for one of them to come to their senses as he backed her deeper into the mews where they would be less likely to be seen.

She pulled back just enough to look at him, her eyes dark with desire. "Don't stop."

The breathless plea shattered his control completely. He captured her mouth again, more urgently this time, his hands exploring her back. His control had evaporated and all that remained was an overwhelming need to have her in his arms.

He backed her against the stable wall, his body caging her in. And she did nothing to discourage him, her fingers fisting in his shirt.

Before he could stop himself, he seized her bottom and pulled her against the hardness of his desire for her. Graham knew one for certain: he would want this woman every day of his life. The tighter that she clung to him, the more his nerves about his inexperience dissipated.

Graham slid his hand up her body, exploring her curves until he reached her breast. She gasped and held onto him tighter. He tenderly squeezed her breast through her dress. With another gasp, she arched her back, pressing her chest against him. The scent of lavender that he'd forever associate with her took over his senses.

Her body responded to his touch, and her nipple hardened beneath his palm. Delighting in her reaction to him, his cock bulged as he teased that precious nipple through the fabric. How he longed to touch her skin, to glide his hands along her softness and warmth. She made the sweetest moans of delight and leaned her head back, exposing her neck to him, and he responded by placing light kisses from her jaw to her neck. His lips trailed along the neckline of her dress, running his tongue just under the edge of her neckline.

"Graham," she whispered.

Hearing his name on her lips in that moment was the loveliest sound he'd ever heard. And he longed to make her do so over and over again.

He ran his hand along her hip and then gripped her skirts, bunching them in his hands to raise them, making her gasp.

"Do you want me to stop?" he ground out.

"No." Then she kissed him again.

He shifted his hand so it was beneath her skirts and then brushed his fingers along her thigh. "Have you ever touched yourself here?" he asked against her lips.

Her cheeks pinkened as she shook her head. "I…I know very little. But I know that I don't want to stop."

He slid his hand higher and fingered the soft, slick folds between them. Then he almost lost his breath entirely.

"Tell me if you change your mind," he murmured, but hoping that she wouldn't. Touching her, his first time to every touch a woman in that way, had consumed him.

He hadn't known what to expect, only what he'd read and

imagined, but the heat and slickness as his fingers slid deeper between her legs was nothing like he'd ever dreamed.

She gasped and clung tighter to his shoulders. "Graham…"

He traced her carefully, his thumb circling the little nub at the peak of her folds, something he learned from the book in his study. Her hips jerked against his hand. The sound she made, something that was a half gasp, half whimper, made him groan.

"Does that—does that feel good?" he asked, trailing kisses along her neck.

"Yes," she whispered, tilted her head to the side, giving him greater access. "Don't stop."

He slid a finger inside her, and the tightness nearly destroyed him. He already imagined what it would be like to truly be inside her. The thought alone made his cock strain painfully against his breeches.

Her body clutched around his finger as he worked it gently, then added another, stretching her, filling her. She moaned, her thighs quivering, hips pressing shamelessly against his hand.

"You feel perfect," he ground out. "Do you feel something building?"

She nodded frantically, breath catching. "Yes—oh, yes—"

He curled his fingers, desperate to wring more of those sounds from her. Her nails dug into his shoulders as her breath grew ragged. He pressed his body tighter against her, his cock rubbing against her hip as he continued to pleasure her. The pressure provided a bit of relief from the way he ached from how hard he was.

His thumb worked over her nub again and again until her whole body trembled. It was the most exhilarating experience he'd ever had in his life.

Suddenly, she cried out and lost herself in his arms, her core clenching around him in hot, pulsing waves.

The sight, the feel, the sound of her release broke him. The intensity of the moment was overwhelming. His cock jerked against the confines of his breeches as he reached his own climax, filling them with his seed as he came with a muffled groan against her throat. He had never come so hard before, and he wasn't sure he'd survive how intense their wedding night would be.

Graham held her tighter as his seed soaked the fabric, praying she wouldn't notice.

She slumped against him, her body still quaking. "I didn't know it could... feel like that," she whispered, flushed and breathless.

Graham eased his hand from her, smoothing her skirts down so she was covered. His heart still hammered with the enormity of what had just happened.

Diana's head rested against his chest. "Graham," she whispered after a long pause, "what was that?"

He swallowed hard, brushing a hand over her hair. "It's called many things." He gave a shaky laugh. "But a climax is one word for it."

"My body felt as though it had no choice but to... to break apart. It was terrifying and wonderful all at the same time."

Graham practically puffed out his chest in pride. "I'll show you more soon."

"Is that...what happens during our wedding night when you enter me?" The innocence of her questions made him feel much better about his own lack of experience. At least they'd learn these things together.

"Yes. I mean...I hope so." He paused, trying to find the right words. "If you want to, that is."

"Anything that feels that good, I must do again." Suddenly her expression shifted to one of concern. "What about you? Was it... pleasurable for you too?"

His seed in his breeches was a sticky reminder of just how much. He cleared his throat. "Every moment of it," he admitted, the truth tumbling out before he could stop it. "Touching you... feeling you... I didn't know it could be like that."

She eyed him curiously. "You didn't?"

He hesitated. He hadn't meant to tell her, but she deserved to know the truth. "Uhh…well…I actually haven't ever been intimate with anyone before. So I'd actually never done…that."

"You haven't?"

He shook his head. "I never wanted to be like my father."

She tenderly cupped his cheek. "I must admit that the thought of you being with anyone that way would drive me mad with jealousy. So I am glad you have never done so. It's always been such an unfair, hypocritical way of men."

"I am inclined to agree." Graham released a silent breath, feeling relieved that he had told her. He didn't need any additional secrets from her. "But I do swear to you, Diana, I'll learn everything I can to please you."

A shy smile touched her lips. "We can learn together."

The words nearly finished him a second time.

CHAPTER EIGHT

Diana

DIANA STOOD BEFORE her mirror, checking her appearance for the dinner party, though her thoughts were elsewhere entirely. They had been since the moment she'd snuck back into her house after the unexpected encounter with Graham.

Her lips still felt tender from Graham's kisses. Her skin still hadn't cooled after the pleasure that he'd introduced her to. Hours had passed, yet she could still feel where his hands had touched her.

She pressed the spot on her throat where he'd kissed her. The memory of the way his lips had moved against her skin brought back that ache between her legs. Somehow, the man she hardly knew had become all could think about.

A soft knock interrupted her reverie. "Come in."

Hannah slipped inside and hurried to close the door. "I'm dreadfully sorry I didn't come sooner, but I didn't see your note in time and then didn't want to alarm Hudson. But I convinced him to come to supper early."

Relief flooded through Diana. She'd been wondering why Hannah hadn't called earlier. "Thank goodness you're here. I feel as though I might burst if I don't tell someone. And we don't have much time before the others arrive."

Her friends would be joining for a small dinner party that

evening. Lydia had arranged it since, in a few days, Diana would be married and hosting her own gatherings. She supposed that was another upside to marriage. Planning events had been something she had enjoyed before Lydia became the lady of the house.

Hannah studied Diana with a concerned expression. "What has happened? Did something happen with the betrothal?"

"I saw Graham this morning. Alone."

Hannah's eyes widened. "Diana—"

"He's teaching me to ride." The words spilled out. "He gave me the most beautiful horse—Luna—and we had a couple lessons."

Hannah's chin nearly hit the floor. "You went to his home unchaperoned? I beg your pardon...you rode a horse? What if your father were to find out?"

"Papa won't have a say in such matters once I'm wed." Diana touched her lips unconsciously, then dropped her hand when she realized what she was doing. "Besides, that wasn't the most scandalous part."

Hannah sank into the chair by the window. "Oh, Diana. What happened?"

"After the lesson, when he was helping me down from the saddle..." Diana lowered her voice. "We kissed. And then he touched me in ways that made me feel things I never knew were possible."

"In what way did he touch you, exactly?"

Color flooded Diana's cheeks, but she pressed on. "His hands... everywhere. My breasts, and then..." She couldn't find the words. "Hannah, I had no idea my body could respond that way. The pleasure was so intense I thought I might faint."

Hannah's eyes widened. "Diana, you didn't let him—"

"Not that. But what we did..." Diana sat heavily on her bed. "I wanted more. I wanted everything. Even now, just thinking about it..." She fanned herself.

Hannah moved to sit beside her, taking her hands. "Are you

all right? He didn't force anything?"

"No, nothing like that. He kept asking if I wanted him to stop." Diana met her friend's worried gaze. "And I don't know why anyone would do anything else but that."

"Oh, my." Hannah squeezed her hand. "You must be careful that he doesn't take advantage of you."

"It's hardly taking advantage when we are to be married." She knew she must look like a silly school girl from the way she grinned. "My intended has proven to be a kind man. He's promised to show me his estate ledgers and agricultural reports so I can help with management. It's even more than I had thought I wanted in a marriage."

"That does sound remarkable," Hannah admitted. "Most men would never—"

"Exactly. He is going to treat me as a true partner. And I already know that he is going to always be honest with me, based on things he's already shared."

Color rose in Diana's cheeks again as she recalled his personal admission about his experience and how much she couldn't wait for them to explore more together. She forced herself to push those thoughts away. "And then there's Luna, she's the most beautiful creature. I've never felt so free as when I was in that saddle. I can hardly wait to ride her again."

"Still, it sounds like you are already becoming rather attached. You must guard your heart. This all happened so quickly and there is still much to learn about the man."

Before Diana could respond, a knock sounded at her door.

"Enter."

Mary cracked the door and poked her head inside. "Lydia sent me to retrieve you both. Other guests have begun to arrive."

"We must join them," Diana said to Hannah, smoothing her skirts. "Not a word about any of this, please."

"Of course not," Hannah replied with a genuine smile.

They made their way downstairs, where Marina, Tabitha, and Juliana were already gathered in the drawing room.

"There you are," Marina called to her. "How are you feeling with everything that is going on?"

"I'm anxious about how different everything will be as a married woman," Diana replied carefully, accepting a glass of wine from a footman.

"I imagine you are," Tabitha said, studying Diana with obvious curiosity. "Though you seem surprisingly... calm for someone facing a forced marriage."

"I'm making the best of the situation," she blurted. "Besides, I find that I like him a great deal. I do believe I'm growing excited about marrying Graham."

Marina scoffed. "You certainly are making the most of things."

Diana's wine glass stilled halfway to her lips. "What do you mean by that?"

Juliana intervened gently. "I think what Marina meant to say is we want to make sure you are going into this marriage with your eyes open. Last week you were considering Lord Ockham as a practical match, and now you seem quite taken with Lord Powis."

"Would you prefer I behaved as if I were being marched to the gallows?" Diana snapped, taking a larger sip of wine than was strictly proper.

"Not at all, but I don't want to see you lose your head over a man you hardly know who compromised you at the first ball of the season," Marina said coolly.

"Marina," Hannah warned.

"I'm merely pointing out that Diana seems remarkably enthusiastic about what should be a rather distressing situation." Marina crossed her arms. "One might almost think she planned it. Similar to her ridiculous plan for Lord Ockham."

"That's enough," Diana said sharply. "I didn't plan anything. But since I must marry him, I see no point in wallowing in misery. Marriage will afford me new freedoms and experiences that I wouldn't have otherwise."

Marina's expression softened. "I am not trying to be cruel. I just want to ensure you keep your head about you. I will rip him apart myself if he steps a toe out of line."

"I have always been practical. More practical than the lot of you." Diana lifted her chin. "But I am marrying the man regardless. We have little choice. And he's offered me a partnership. Respect. He's already promised to share estate management with me and wants my input as he makes decisions about his holdings."

That surprised them all. Even Marina looked taken aback.

"He's allowing you access to everything?" Juliana asked.

"We'll go over all of it together. He values my knowledge of such matters." Diana couldn't hide her excitement about this prospect.

Tabitha shifted on her feet. "I hope he doesn't have financial concerns. I heard that his cousin had quite a habit of running up gambling debts."

Diana froze for a moment, recalling Elias's concern that Graham had trapped her on purpose for her dowry. But she couldn't believe he would do that. "I shall see soon enough. He promised me that I would get to go over everything with him."

"It's one thing to make such promises," Marina said carefully. "Men often say what they think women wish to hear."

"Graham isn't like that. He is one of the most honest men that you shall ever meet."

"You've known him less than a week," Marina pointed out. "How can you possibly know what he's like?"

The question hit its mark because Diana couldn't refute it entirely.

"I can't," she admitted. "But I have to trust my instincts."

"Your instincts led you into a dark garden with a stranger," Marina said bluntly. "Perhaps they need refinement."

"You overstep, Marina," Hannah said firmly. "What's done is done. Diana will marry Lord Powis, and as her friends, we should support her."

"I am supporting her," Marina protested. "By reminding her not to mistake physical attraction or empty promises for something more."

Before Diana could respond, she heard her father Elias and Hudson approaching.

Elias's expression was thunderous as he focused on Diana. "Sister. I trust you've had a pleasant day?"

The pointed way he said it made Diana's stomach drop. "Perfectly pleasant, thank you."

"Just how pleasant? Because we had a most illuminating conversation with Lord Ashworth this afternoon." Elias's voice was dangerously quiet. "It seems you were observed leaving Lord Powis's residence today."

Diana felt the weight of all her friends' gazes, and worst of all, her father's. "I was simply—"

"Simply what?" Elias snapped. "Compromising yourself further? Making this matter more precarious than it already was?"

"Or perhaps Lord Powis is taking liberties he has no right to?" Hudson chimed in.

Both Diana and Hannah flashed him a murderous expression to indicate that he should mind his business.

"He didn't bed me, if that is what you aim to ask in front of everyone," Diana practically snarled back at her brother, fisting her hands at her sides.

"Daughter," her father started, his tone commanding the room. "You will not visit him again without a chaperone. Is that understood?"

Diana's temper flared. "You cannot dictate—"

"I can and I will. You're my daughter and still under protection, and I won't have you become the subject of further gossip." His voice softened slightly. "Diana, I know this situation isn't ideal, but you cannot make it worse by behaving recklessly."

"How is getting to know my future husband reckless?" She almost stomped her foot, but stopped herself since a childish tantrum wasn't likely to help them see her as a woman who was an adult and about to be married.

"Because your actions impact this entire family," Elias interjected. "This isn't just about you. You went off in the dark with the man doing God knows what and the rest of us have to ensure that we aren't all ruined because of it."

Diana had enough of her brother's high-handed tone. "Were you thinking of the implications to this family when you were quite improper with Lydia in our family home? Let's not pretend that you weren't a known rake gallivanting about town less than a year ago, brother."

Elias's face turned redder than she'd ever seen him. "How dare—"

"Silence," their father boomed. "Both of you are out of line and this conversation ends now. Our family has always been built on love and respect. And we will extend that respect to Diana's future husband." He locked eyes with Diana.

Tears pricked Diana's eyes, regretting what she said to her brother. Of course she loved him, and when he wasn't being an odious bear, he was one of her favorite people. And she was delighted that he and Lydia had found each other.

But his days of speaking to her as his immature little sister had to come to an end. Soon she would be a married woman, and possibly a mother not long after that.

The dinner that followed was strained. The conversation stilted as everyone danced around the obvious tension. Diana found herself distracted, thinking about how concerned her family and friends were for the situation. She was being a bit idealistic compared to her usual practical nature. Was she truly being foolish?

But then she'd recall how tender he'd been with him. And how beautiful and wonderful he made her feel. And her thoughts were nothing but a muddled mess.

By the time her friends departed that evening, Diana felt wrung out and confused, caught between desire and doubt.

Lydia found her in the drawing room afterward, staring into

the dying fire.

"Are you all right, dearest?"

Diana sighed heavily. "Everyone thinks I'm making a terrible mistake."

"They're worried about you. This has all happened so quickly." Lydia settled beside her on the sofa. "And I suppose you have a point about your brother and how our marriage came about."

"I shouldn't have said that. Please forgive me."

Lydia reached for her hand and clasped it. "Your brother can be a trying man. No one knows that better than me. But he is fierce when it comes to protecting his family."

Diana squeezed her sister-in-law's hand tight. "I know. But I don't know what you all expect of me. I'm told I have no choice but to marry him, and then when I'm feeling content about marrying him, I'm told that's wrong, too."

"You are allowed to feel whatever it is you want. Only you know your own mind and heart."

Her heart. She hadn't considered her heart being involved in her marriage. She had never thought about love at all. But perhaps it wasn't one of those things that happened in an instant, it was something that grew from partnership, respect, and honesty. Even if the attraction she had for him had been instantaneous. But that wasn't love.

Even though every time she closed her eyes, she could still feel Graham's touch, and recall every detail about everything they shared.

But did it even truly matter what she felt? There was no turning back now.

CHAPTER NINE

Graham

GRAHAM STOOD BEFORE the altar of St. George's. His hands were clasped tightly behind his back forcing himself to keep his chin high as he faced their wedding guest. The church was filled with faces he didn't even recognize, all eager to witness the marriage that had been the talk of the *ton* for the past week.

Matt stood beside him as his best man, occasionally murmuring reassurances that Graham barely heard over the pounding of his own heart. And his guilt. The weight of what he was about to do…going against his plan to marry solely for love. The more he learned about Diana, the more he was convinced that love might have even struck if he could let himself admit it. But was that even enough when he was binding Diana to him while hiding debts that could destroy them both?

The guests began tittering and Graham saw Diana entering the church on her father's arm. He was unable to breathe watching her walk toward him. She wore a blue silk gown that brought out the deep blue of her eyes. Her golden hair was swept up, revealing the elegant line of her neck that he longed to kiss again.

Their eyes met across the length of the aisle, and Graham saw his own nervous anticipation reflected in her sapphire gaze. She offered him a small, private smile that made his chest tighten with something dangerously close to hope. Something deep inside nagged at him that she was the one that fate had brought them together. But it was dangerous to allow himself to believe that.

When the Earl of Snowdon placed Diana's hand in Graham's, his grip was firm, his message clear—protect her, or else. Graham gulped in response.

The ceremony passed in a blur. Graham heard himself speaking the vows, promising to love, honor, and cherish. Words that should have been mere formality but felt like so much more as he looked into Diana's eyes. Because he meant them.

When she repeated her own vows, her voice was steady and clear, though he felt the slight tremor in her hands as he slipped the ring onto her finger.

"You may kiss your bride," the vicar announced.

Graham cupped Diana's face gently, aware of the dozens of eyes upon them. He meant it to be a brief, proper kiss for their audience. But when their lips met, Diana made a soft sound that nearly undid him. He deepened the kiss for just a moment before remembering where they were and pulling back.

The congregation erupted in polite applause, but Graham barely heard it. Diana's eyes were dark, her lips slightly parted, and he knew she was remembering their encounter in the stables just as vividly as he was.

The wedding breakfast at her family's home passed in a whirlwind of congratulations and a few hushed whispers. Graham endured endless comments about the "whirlwind romance" and "love at first sight," each one making his guilt grow heavier.

He caught snippets of one conversation when he sought another glass of champagne that made his jaw clench.

"…rather convenient for him, inheriting a title and immediately securing an heiress…"

He didn't think Diana had heard it. The entire day her chin was high and her smile never wavered. But Graham saw the tension in her shoulders, and when her fingers sought his to grip his hand it all truly hit him. They were married. She was his forever.

Diana leaned closer. "How much longer must we endure this?"

"Not much longer," he promised, squeezing her hand. "We'll leave for our townhouse soon."

"Our townhouse," she repeated softly. "I like the sound of that."

Elias approached them interrupting the moment, and Graham regretted not throwing Diana over his shoulder and leaving already. "Powis. A word?"

Graham nodded, releasing Diana's hand reluctantly and followed Elias to a quiet corner.

"I still don't trust you," Elias said bluntly. "But Diana seems… content. For her sake, I hope you prove worthy of my sister."

"I intend to." And he meant that. All would be as soon as he resolved this business with Rothwell, his full focus would be on Diana.

"See that you do."

Graham nodded in agreement, and then moved back to Diana's side. "I believe we have stayed as long as we must."

"I have to admit that you two certainly make a most striking pair," a female voice said, interrupting their plan to escape.

Lady Harrowby.

"Thank you for coming, Lady Harrowby. It's always lovely to see you." Diana possessed all the grace and charm to assume the role of his countess. She was far more equipped for the title than he was. Graham bowed to the woman before she locked eyes with him. "I don't see any of your family present, my boy. I was aware your father passed, but did your mother not wish to join you in town?"

Graham slowly shook his head. "She will arrive in town in another week or so."

The woman's brow furrowed. "I do hope she is all right."

It was a curious response. "She is well as far as I know."

"I won't keep you. I know you're only staying long enough to be respectful to your guests." The woman gave a knowing smirk and nodded to each of them before walking away. She was an odd duck. But it was their wedding day and his new bride was far more important than deciphering the dragon of the *ton*.

They set out hand in hand to seek out Diana's family. The goodbyes were emotional, even though Diana would just be a few blocks over. At least for the time being until they ventured to their country home.

"You know where we are if you need us," her father said quietly, his eyes finding Graham's over Diana's head. The warning was clear.

The carriage ride to Graham's townhouse was silent but charged with awareness. Diana sat beside him, close enough that he could smell her lavender scent, and she kept shifting in her seat.

"Are you all right?" he asked finally.

"We're married," she said, as if testing the words.

He gulped. "That wasn't an answer. Are you all right?"

She turned to look at him fully. "I'm…nervous."

"About…intimate matters?" He stumbled over his words.

"No," she said quickly, almost as if he'd grown a second head. "Not that. Not at all. This is just all an enormous amount of change. I don't know what my life will look like each day, or if you will eat supper with me every night, or what my bed chamber looks like, or—"

He reached out and clasped her chin so she looked at him.

"Why don't we take things a day at a time? I have hardly been an earl for a fortnight, and here we are married. Let's just go on as we wish."

Something in her expression softened. "Did you get the estate ledgers?"

"Yes. But might we celebrate our marriage in the more traditional sense and save the ledgers for tomorrow?" He leaned closer and brushed his lips against her ear. "Because I have thought of little else since…"

He placed a few kisses behind her ear.

The carriage rolled to a stop, putting an end to such notions. But that was to be expected given they didn't have a long ride. The staff was assembled to greet their new mistress. Graham watched with pride as Diana charmed each one, remembering names and making them feel at ease.

Mrs. Mitchell, the housekeeper, showed Diana to the suite of rooms that adjoined Graham's. Graham followed, hovering in the doorway as Diana took in the room after Mrs. Mitchell had departed.

"It's lovely." She ran her fingers along the carved bedpost.

"You can change anything you like," Graham said, but then regretted it since he wasn't ready for such expenditures. But he assured himself it wouldn't always be that way.

"Are you in need of rest?" Graham asked, though every fiber of his being wanted her.

"Graham." Diana moved closer to him. "I do not wish to rest."

His body was aflame with want. He was seconds away from pulling her to him. "I didn't want to presume—"

"You're my husband now." She reached up to caress his face. "And I…I want you."

Graham caught her hand, forcing himself to take things slow as he pressed his lips to her palm. "Diana, are you certain?"

"I've been dreaming of this," she admitted, her cheeks flushed. "About what…being with you fully would be like."

Graham groaned, this time he pulled her against him and walked her toward his bed chamber through the adjoining door. Once they were inside, he kicked the door closed. "You don't want to know the ways I've imagined you."

"And what if I do?" She was already working at his cravat. "I'm allowed to be as wanton as I wish as a married woman."

Somehow he had managed to marry the most perfect woman that had ever existed. He kissed her with all of the intensity that had been building the last couple of days he'd spent apart from her, pouring all his longing and guilt and hope into it. She responded eagerly, her arms winding around his neck.

"Help me remove my dress," she whispered against his mouth, turning to present her back to him.

Graham forced himself to take a deep breath as he worked through the long row of tiny buttons. With each one undone, he revealed more of her skin, and he couldn't resist pressing his lips to the nape of her neck.

Diana shivered. "Graham…"

He helped her step out of the gown, then her stays and chemise, until she stood before him in nothing but her stockings and slippers. Graham forgot how to breathe.

"You're magnificent," he managed.

Diana's blush spread down her chest, but she didn't try to cover herself. Instead, she began removing his coats and shirt. He brushed her hand away when she started to unbutton his breeches. He would have to pace himself to have any chance of making the experience what she deserved for it to be. And that meant his pants needed to remain on for the time being.

Graham pulled the blankets back and then lifted her onto the bed, settling beside her. The feel of her bare skin against his nearly undid him completely.

"I've been told that the first time might hurt," Diana said quietly.

"I'll be gentle. I promise." He kissed her, letting his hands explore her body. "If you want me to stop at any point—"

"I won't." She arched against him as his fingers found her breast. "I want this. I want you."

Graham kissed his way down her throat. His hands explored her curves, learning every dip and swell of her body. When his mouth closed over her nipple, Diana arched off the bed with a sharp cry.

"So responsive," he murmured against her skin, switching to the other breast while his fingers teased the bud he'd just abandoned. He was still quite thankful that he'd found that book. "Do you like this?"

"Graham," she gasped, tangling her fingers in his hair. "Yes… please…"

He knew what she needed. His hand slid down her stomach, through the nest of curls between her thighs, finding her slick already. Diana's hips bucked as he circled that sensitive bud he'd discovered before.

"You're so wet," he groaned, sliding a finger inside her. The tight clench of her core made his cock throb painfully. "So perfect."

Diana was writhing beneath him, her thighs spreading wider as he worked his fingers in and out, moving them in different ways to see what she responded to the most. "More," she demanded, and he loved watching her enjoy herself. "I want more."

Graham added a second finger, stretching her carefully while his thumb continued circling.

He let her moan and move against his hand, and then withdrew his fingers.

"Why did you stop?" she whined, pushing the hair from her face.

Instead of answering her, he came onto his knees and kissed his way down her body until his head was perfectly positioned between her legs.

"Graham, what are you—oh!"

His mouth was on her, tongue exploring her seam with such care that he hoped it made up for his inexperience. The first time that he plunged his tongue inside of her, he was hooked. He was already addicted to the taste of her and the way she trembled and gasped his name. It was intoxicating.

"Graham!" Diana gripped his hair, holding him in place. "That's… I didn't even… oh God…"

He sucked gently on that sensitive nub while sliding his fingers back inside her, and in only a matter of moments, Diana was moaning and bucking on the bed, her thighs clamping around his head as she practically convulsed from her orgasm.

Graham kissed his way back up her body, his cock so hard it was beyond painful. He needed her more than he'd ever needed anything in his life.

"That was…incredible," she whispered, then placed several light kisses across his lips. "I want you inside me."

He climbed from the bed and removed his breeches. She watched him, her eyes widening when his cock jutted up proudly.

"I…You are…Your size, I mean," she started.

Graham climbed back onto the bed, hovering over her. He kissed her for several minutes, massaging her tongue with his. Kissing her with an equal amount of need and tenderness.

He broke the kiss and looked into her eyes. "I am made to fit inside of you," he reassured her. "But if you aren't ready…"

She wrapped her arms around his neck, holding him so close their hearts beat together. "I'm ready."

He kissed her again as he positioned himself at her entrance, the head of his cock sliding through her folds to reach her opening. They both groaned at the sensation.

"Look at me," he commanded softly. "I've got you."

Their gazes locked as he pressed forward slowly. Diana's breath hitched, her body tensing at the intrusion.

"Just breathe," he whispered, stilling with just the tip inside. "Tell me if it's too much."

He meant what he said, that he would stop if she commanded. But he prayed that she wouldn't. Because he was going to go mad if he couldn't be inside of her.

"Don't stop," she gasped, her nails digging into his shoulders. "Please don't stop."

Graham pressed forward inch by torturous inch, sweat beading on his forehead from the effort of going slow when all he wanted to do was bury himself to the hilt inside of his wife. She was so tight, so hot, gripping him and pulling him inside. When he was halfway in, Diana instinctively wrapped her legs around his waist and his entire length had entered her in one swift motion.

She twinged and her face contorted for a moment. Then her eyelids grew heavy as her legs tightened around him. Graham's arms trembled as he held himself still, giving her time to adjust.

"Are you all right?" he asked her, placing kisses at the corner of her lips.

"Yes," she panted.

He withdrew slowly, then thrust back in, setting a slow rhythm. Nothing had ever felt so wonderful, and perfect. And now that he'd experienced it, he'd never be able to be without her.

"You are mine," he ground out, increasing the speed of his thrusts.

She nodded and moaned, eyes clenched shut and pushed her body against him to meet him when he entered her.

Graham supported himself with one arm and cupped her cheek with his other hand while he continued the rhythm that he set. "Look at me."

She opened her eyes and he saw everything he could have ever hoped for there.

"Say you are mine," he commanded.

"I'm yours." She released a steady stream of moans. "I'm all yours."

Graham lost what remained of his control. He hitched her leg higher over his hip, changing the angle, and drove into her with increasing force. Diana's cries grew louder, her nails raking down his back.

"Yes," she cried.

He could feel her beginning to tighten around him. Determined to bring her over the edge once more before he lost himself, he slipped his hand between them, his thumb finding her sensitive nub.

"Come for me," he growled against her ear.

Diana's back arched and she clamped down on him as she came with a scream. The feeling of her pulsing around him made Graham unable to fight his own release. He pushed himself all the way in, spilling everything he had deep inside her, whispering her name over and over.

Graham collapsed beside her on the bed, pulling Diana against him as they both struggled to catch their breath.

He removed himself from the bed and grabbed a cloth and wet it in the wash basin. Then he used the damp cloth to clean between her legs, then used the cloth on himself.

He tossed the cloth aside and then climbed back into bed with her. She nestled against him as if it were the most natural thing in the world. As if it was the way they would be for all of time. Diana's head rested on his chest, her fingers tracing patterns on his skin.

"Was it… was I…?" Graham couldn't finish the question.

Diana lifted her head to look at him. "It was perfect. You were perfect."

Relief flooded through him. "You were extraordinary."

She smiled, that dimpled smile that made his heart race. As she settled back against him, Graham stared at the ceiling, his guilt warring with an overwhelming flood of emotion for the woman in his arms.

"Graham?" Diana's voice was drowsy. "What are you thinking about?"

"You," he said, which was true. "Just you."

She hummed contentedly, pressing a kiss to his chest. "I think I'm going to like being married to you."

And he had a feeling he was going to love being married to her. Emphasis on love. He was quite certain she already held his heart in her hand. "Diana—"

But her breathing had already evened out in sleep. Graham held her closer, vowing silently that he would fix everything, and once he did, he'd tell her how he felt. That he was quite certain that regardless of the circumstances that resulted in their marriage. That he was utterly and completely in love with his wife.

But he had to protect her first by dealing with Rothwell. And the sooner the better.

CHAPTER TEN

Diana

DIANA SLIPPED FROM the bed as quietly as possible, not wanting to wake Graham. She hadn't expected that they'd share a bed together the entire night. But the night was spent dozing off after the exquisite bliss of a climax and then one of them waking the other to do it again. Her body ached, but it was well worth it. She'd tired out muscles that she'd never known existed.

She studied her sleeping husband in the morning light streaming through the curtains. His dark hair was thoroughly mussed, one arm flung across the space where she'd been lying. Even in sleep, he looked satisfied—almost smug. As well he should be, given how many times he'd made her cry out his name throughout all hours of the night.

It was clear why women were discouraged from knowing about such pleasures before marriage. Because now that she'd had her husband, she certainly didn't want to stop.

Her skin heated again from recalling how wanton she had been in their marriage bed. The way he'd turned her onto her stomach and taken her from behind, so deep she'd seen stars and knew she'd beg for him to do so again. The way he'd pulled her atop him, teaching her to ride him as she'd ridden Luna, praising her when she found the rhythm that pleased them both. And the exploration they did with their mouths…

And she knew she was a frightful sight after the most exciting night of her life.

"Where do you think you're going?" Graham mumbled into his pillow.

"To order a bath. I'm rather in need of one."

"Mmm." He cracked one eye open. "Come back to bed after."

"I think you are missing the point of the bath, husband." Diana giggled then leaned down and kissed his shoulder, before slipping into her chemise and venturing to her adjoining chambers. For a moment, she paused and pondered how affectionate acts seemed natural already. Easy, even.

She rang for Mary, and immediately asked for hot water to be brought up for the bath.

While she waited, she examined herself in the mirror. Her lips were swollen from kisses, her neck marked with the places where his mouth had been, and her hair in complete disarray. She looked thoroughly debauched…and quite satisfied.

The servants arrived, filling the copper tub with steaming water and Mary left lavender oils and fresh towels. Diana dismissed them, then pulled off her chemise and tested the water with her toe.

"Starting without me?"

She turned to find Graham leaning against the doorframe, completely naked and given the state of his manhood…aroused.

"You appeared content in your bed," she said, trying not to stare at his naked body now that she could see him even better in the daylight. Yet his gaze wasn't focused on her eyes.

"Our bed." He slunk toward her, and captured her hands in his. "I think we have demonstrated the necessity of sharing a bed."

Her heart fluttered in her chest. She almost thought she might wake at any moment to find that it all had been a dream. She blinked her eyes closed and when she opened them, she was elated to find that it was all real.

Graham helped her into the tub, and Diana sighed as the hot water soothed her aching muscles. Then he climbed in behind her, pulling her back against his chest.

"This is heaven," she murmured, relaxing into his embrace.

"No," he corrected her, sudsing up her arms. "Heaven was last night. This is merely pleasant."

Diana laughed. "Merely pleasant? You wound me, husband."

"Then let me make amends." His soapy hands moved to her breasts, massaging them gently. "Better?"

"Much." She arched into his touch as his thumbs circled her nipples. Despite her soreness, desire began to stir again.

Graham took his time washing every inch of her, his touch alternating between soothing and arousing. When his hand slipped between her thighs, Diana gasped.

"Still sore?" he murmured against her ear.

"Yes, but—" She lost her words as his fingers found that sensitive bundle of nerves, circling gently.

"Let me make you feel good," he coaxed, his touch light. "Just relax against me and I'll do everything."

Diana melted into his chest as he worked her body with maddening slowness. He massaged her thighs and brushed his fingers over her sensitive nub. He kissed and licked along her ear and neck. The pleasure built gradually and she had never felt more relaxed, yet more aware of every sensation in her body. She tensed just as she was about to fall over the edge of the building pleasure that he teased her with for what felt like an hour.

"That's it," he encouraged. "Just let go."

She came with a soft cry, the climax gentle but intense, lasting for what felt like minutes. Graham held her through it, pressing kisses upon her temple.

"Better?" he asked when she could breathe again.

"Much," she sighed, then realized he was still hard against her back. "What about you?"

"I feel quite confident that I'll get my turn later, if last night was any indication." He reached for the soap again. "Now let me wash your hair."

Graham massaged her scalp, working the soap through her long tresses with infinite care.

"You're going to spoil me," she murmured.

"That's the plan." He rinsed her hair with fresh water from the pitcher.

Once her hair was rinsed, Diana shifted in the tub so she faced him. She took the soap and lathered her hands and then went to work massaging his chest and shoulders, placing kisses on his neck and jaw when his head fell back over the side of the tub.

"I should have married you a long time ago," he teased.

"Too bad I couldn't have followed you into a garden during my first season," Diana replied, running her soapy hands down his torso.

He captured her mouth in a lingering kiss. "We'll just make up for lost time."

Diana's hands slid lower until her fingertips brushed the base of his cock. He gave a sharp intake of breath, his eyes opening to meet hers. She could see the desire in them.

Her lips curved with mischief. "You've been very attentive, husband. It seems only fair that I return the favor."

"Diana…" His voice was a low warning, but he did nothing to stop her. Instead, he rested his arms on the edge of the tub and watched. His cock was hard as she wrapped her fingers around his manhood.

The soap made her hand glide easily, and she loved watching the way that his expression shifted to need from her touch. She stroked slowly at first, watching his head lean back against the rim of the tub, throat working as he swallowed hard.

He released a low growl and gripped the sides of the tub. She tightened her hold and varied her speed, delighting in every moan he gave her. She must be doing something right.

"Is this good for you?" she whispered, leaning closer to kiss his throat. She had never felt bolder and more beautiful in her life knowing that she controlled his pleasure the way she did.

His laugh was shaky. "Far better than good."

She quickened her strokes, fascinated by the way his chest heaved and the way the muscles in his neck flexed. When she brushed her thumb over the sensitive head, he cursed softly, his entire body tensing beneath her hand.

"Diana—" His plea broke off as he shot his seed into her hand, swirling in the water. He groaned as he put his hand over hers to still her movement.

She smiled, reveling in her triumph. "There. Now we're even."

He caught her chin and kissed her hard. "I can't think of a better way to start the day."

Graham helped her out of the tub and then dried them both. He then helped her into the silk wrapper that Mary left. "I'm going to have breakfast sent up."

She followed him back into his chamber where he donned a burgundy banyan before reaching for the bell pull. Within a quarter hour later, they had breakfast trays with eggs, bacon, fresh bread, jam, and strong tea set out on the small table in the shared parlor in their suite.

Once they were alone, Diana eagerly arranged a plate for herself. "I'm famished."

"I can't imagine why," Graham said with a wicked grin, buttering a piece of bread for her.

They both ate as if they had been starving, making little conversation between bites. Diana couldn't remember the last time that she had ever been so hungry.

"I have something for you," Graham said once they'd finished eating. He retrieved a large box from his wardrobe and set it on the bed.

"What is it?"

"Open it and see."

Diana lifted the lid and instantly ran her fingers along the fabric. Inside lay a beautiful deep emerald green riding habit. It was more serviceable than flashy, which was perfect.

"Graham," she gushed. "Thank you. This is perfect!"

"I want you to feel comfortable as you build your confidence riding your horse."

Diana placed a chaste kiss on his cheek. "I'm going to dress in it now."

"Graham shook his head. "I supposed I had better dress, too."

"Yes," she exclaimed. "I want my lesson."

After they dressed, the pair made their way out to the mews, and Diana couldn't help but blush at the memory of the last time she had been there, before her father practically locked her away until she had married.

Diana immediately went to Luna, who appeared excited to see her. "Ready for another lesson, girl?"

The groom approached and saddled Luna for her, and then saddled Midnight. Graham helped her mount her horse, and then he leaped into his own saddle. For the next hour, Graham instructed her while he rode beside her and Luna. Diana's confidence grew with each loop they made as Graham coached her through walking, then trotting, then the terrifying joy of her first canter.

"Excellent!" Graham called as she brought Luna back for a walk. Her heart was pounding. "You're a natural, Diana."

When he finally helped her dismount, she couldn't believe that she had just done that. And wasn't certain how she had gone her whole life without being allowed to do so.

"That was incredible," she said, throwing her arms around his neck. "I can't believe I did it!"

"You did wonderfully." He held her close. "Soon we'll have you riding in Hyde Park. It's only a matter of time before your father and brother find out and have my head."

"Papa is back in the country." Diana said, placing a quick kiss on his cheek. "And I don't care what Elias thinks."

"It isn't you that he will be cross with." Graham released her and motioned toward the house for them to return inside. "Well, perhaps that isn't true. But he can't plant you a facer."

She took his arm and allowed him to lead her back through the garden. Life had become almost perfect. She had a handsome, passionate husband who she hadn't even realized she needed. And she was learning to ride a horse. All that was to take over the management of their house and advise Graham on the management of their estates and life would be complete. Diana touched her stomach, acknowledging that a babe is what would truly make their life complete. She would have it all. More than most women of the *ton* were afforded.

And as unlikely as it was, and as much as she wanted to guard her heart, she was starting to allow the possibility of love to creep in. The more time she spent with Graham, the more that she couldn't imagine not being with him. How she couldn't wait for each day of their marriage to build their life together. It went beyond attraction and infatuation. But was it love?

Diana shook off the thought, deciding that she didn't need to name her feelings at present. They had just married and she needn't rush things. Either way, they would be married for the rest of their lives.

"Ready for those ledgers now?" Graham asked, pulling her from her thoughts.

"You know the way to a woman's heart," Diana teased. "Horses and account books."

And her heart flipped again. "And the household accounts, too."

⇒⇒⇒⟨⟨⟨⟨

AFTER A LIGHT luncheon, they settled in Graham's study with ledgers spread across the desk. Diana felt eager to dive into everything. This was what she excelled at, what made her feel useful and valued.

"Shall we start with this one?" Diana asked, opening the first ledger.

"Of course," Graham said. As she looked up, she saw him tuck a few pieces of parchment into his drawer, then he picked up a different ledger.

Diana spread the accompanying documents before her, immediately losing herself in the columns of figures. After a few minutes, she caught Graham's attention. "The yields are far below what they should be for that acreage."

"What would you suggest?"

"It's likely the drainage needs updating, and they should rotate the crops differently." She made notes on a fresh piece of parchment, organizing them by the name of the property and what plan she had for each one. "If you implemented these changes, you could increase profits by at least thirty percent within two years."

"You are brilliant," he said, thumbing through one of the ledgers from the stack.

Diana completed the same review for each of the entailed properties. With her plans, the profits would be much higher than they had been. She intended to broach the subject of her discussing the matters herself with each estate manager. Then she organized the ledgers and papers and set them aside. "Now what about your unentailed properties?"

A curious expression crossed Graham's face. She wasn't certain what to make of it, but he paused for a moment and then he handed her some of the ledgers that he had been thumbing through.

She took the first one and began to organize her notes the same way for these on a different piece of parchment. "This one has a lot of potential," she said, wondering if he was concerned about the state of the properties.

"Oh," he said, rising from his chair to stand over her shoulder. "How much do you think the property is worth?"

"I would say around forty thousand pounds based on the annual earnings. If you made some changes to increase the yields, possibly closer to sixty."

"That much?" he said, seemingly surprised. "And that is if you were to sell it?"

She eyed him, wondering what he was about. "I wouldn't sell these properties. They are worth far more to keep as investments."

Diana thought she might have seen something flicker in his expression, but if it did, it was gone as quickly as she saw it.

"I see," he grumbled. "What about the next one?"

"Give me a moment," she said, shooing him back to his seat.

After several minutes, she had a good picture of things. "This one is quite valuable. It hasn't been producing as well as it should, but even still it would be worth around eighty thousand pounds. I have a massive list of things we are going to change at this one and it's going to make a significant income."

Graham released a sigh of relief, which was even more curious. Although, she knew he didn't know much about estate management.

"May I see the information for that property and the last one?" he asked. "I want to take a look for myself and see what I can learn."

Diana focused on the next property, then after she read the first few lines she immediately knew that there was an issue. "These mortgage payments on the Yorkshire property seem unusually high. When were these terms negotiated? And what's the current principal balance?"

Graham's jaw tightened. "That's an old arrangement from my cousin. Nothing that requires immediate attention. I can take that one."

"But surely I should understand all outstanding obligations?" Diana pressed, already calculating the interest that the property was costing them. "If the terms are unfavorable, we might consider refinancing or—"

"Diana." Graham's voice was gentle but firm as he motioned to her. "Let me see that one."

She handed it to him, dumbfounded at whatever the devil he

was about.

He looked through the first few pages and then closed the ledger and set it aside with the others. "Let's focus on the properties that offer immediate improvement opportunities first. This one can wait."

There was something in his tone that she didn't like. "Graham, I need to see the complete financial picture to give you proper advice. What are the total liquid assets? The current debt obligations? I can't recommend selling or improving properties without knowing our available capital."

"Of course," he said, forcing a smile that didn't reach his eyes. "We'll get to all of that. Today, let us—"

"No." Something seemed off, but she wasn't certain what it was. "You told me that I would be permitted to review everything and help with the decisions."

She reached for the stack of correspondence he'd been guarding, but Graham's hand closed over hers.

"And you shall," he said, pulling her from her chair and seating her on his lap. "Right now, I need you."

He captured her lips in a deep kiss, his tongue immediately meeting hers. His hand found his way beneath her skirts, running his fingers along her thighs.

Diana gasped against his mouth as his fingers teased higher, stroking the tender place that already ached for him. Graham rose, lifting her effortlessly onto an empty edge of the desk.

"It would seem that you need me, too," he said, spreading her legs wider so that he stood between them.

"Graham—" she moaned, unable to deny that she was in such dire need of him.

His mouth claimed hers again and then his hands were pushing her skirts up around her waist. He gripped her hips and pulled her closer to the edge.

Diana clutched at his shoulders, her breath catching as he pressed into her in one long, slow thrust. She cried out at the fullness, her body still tender yet wanting him. He swallowed the sound with his kiss, grinding harder and deeper.

"I'll never get enough of you," he ground out. He set a punishing rhythm, driving into her with force enough to rock the desk. She clung to him, nails digging into his back as he brought her closer to the pinnacle she knew was coming.

"Graham—oh God—"

"That's it," he groaned against her ear, holding her tight while he took her. "Come for me. I want to feel you come."

At that moment, she couldn't hold back any longer and her orgasm overtook her entire body. She threw her head back, her body shaking as intense pleasure overtook her. He thrust one hard final time before shifting to small pulses as his heart pounded against her through his moan.

For a few minutes, they stayed locked together, his chest pressed to hers. Diana wrapped her arms around his neck, basking in the aftermath of her climax.

But as his breathing steadied, she felt it again—that faint shift in him. His hands lingered on her waist, but there was tension in his shoulders, and something different in his eyes when he finally looked at her. It was some emotion mixed with guilt, perhaps.

Diana kissed him once more, and he signed into the kiss. Perhaps she imagined it. Perhaps she was simply overwrought from the day, from the riding lesson, from the way he'd just taken her on the desk.

She traced his jaw with her fingertips and she did her best to push aside her suspicions. As much as they nagged at her.

Running her hands over his shoulders, she was choosing for now not to press him further. It could very well be nothing. He had been honest with her thus far, and she had no reason to believe otherwise.

He had better not be hiding anything or lying. Because she had already failed to guard her heart and now it belonged to him.

CHAPTER ELEVEN
Graham

GRAHAM STARED AT the papers spread across his study desk, Diana's neat handwriting with her recommendations staring back at him. Her analysis was brilliant and just what he needed. She'd identified exactly which unentailed properties would fetch the best prices so he knew which ones he'd put up for sale. And with her recommendations for improvements their other properties would yield the highest returns, which would secure their future for years to come and keep Diana in the life she deserved.

And keep him from meeting his end at the hands of Rothwell, leaving Diana to face a fate he couldn't bear to imagine.

She'd essentially solved his problem for him without even knowing it. And the guilt of misleading and using her that way was eating away at him. But he had to ensure she was safe from the situation his dead cousin had put him in.

He picked up her notes on the Somerset property. Forty thousand pounds, she'd estimated for the current value. That was almost enough to pay Rothwell. And if he sold the eighty-thousand-pound property as well, then he would be able to pay Rothwell, pay off the mortgaged properties and fill his coffers to ensure Diana could implement her improvements for the remaining properties.

But she'd also said they shouldn't sell, that the properties were worth more as investments. How could he tell her that investment returns meant nothing if Rothwell's men came calling?

The decision had been made. He'd already written the necessary letters and had Mitchell post them. The properties would be listed for immediate sale. And it would solve everything.

A knock at the door made him quickly shuffle the papers into a drawer. "Enter."

Mitchell appeared. "Mr. Rothwell to see you, my lord. He says you're expecting him."

Graham's stomach clenched. "Bring him here."

He needed to deal with the man and then get rid of him as quickly as possible. He wasn't certain how would explain his presence to Diana, and he didn't want to lie about yet another thing.

"Lord Powis." The man's voice was riddled with condescension as he swept into the room. "I thought I would check on your progress."

"I should have his funds within our agreed upon deadline."

"The full amount?"

"Yes." Graham kept his voice steady despite the way his pulse raced. He needed the man to leave before Diana saw him.

"Excellent. And might I ask about your lovely new countess? I trust married life is agreeing with you both?"

Graham shot up from his chair and fisted his hands at his sides at the mention of Diana. "My wife is none of your concern."

"Everything is my concern until I have my payment." Rothwell adjusted his gloves. "I am prepared to deduct five thousand pounds from what you owe…if you allow me full access to your wife for a night."

Graham's entire body tensed and in that moment he lost control. He flung himself from around the desk and drew back his arm, planting his fist directly into the man's face with everything he had. "Do not dare to mention my wife again."

Rothwell wobbled on his feet and then covered his cheek with his hand. Then he started laughing. "So you care about the chit?"

"Leave my house!" Graham roared, his entire body shaking from rage and his desire to rip the man apart with his bare hands. "I'll summon you when I have the funds ready, and do not return here."

"You've got more fight in you than that sniveling cousin of yours. I'll give you that," Rothwell said, starting for the door. Just as he was on the other side, he popped his head back in. "But be certain your payment arrives on time. Or else I'll make you watch while I have my way with your wife before I put a bullet in your head."

Then he closed the door.

Graham shifted on his feet, deciding what to do next. His good sense left his body and he charged after the man, ready to take out every bit of his fury on the man's face. But just as he flung the door open, Diana was on the other side.

"Graham?"

Rothwell was nowhere to be seen. And Graham drank in the sight of her. She was dressed in a soft blue morning gown that made her eyes sparkle from the way she looked at him. And he never wanted that sparkle to vanquish.

He wrapped his arms around her and pulled her close, the rage that bubbled within him shifting into fear. All of this was to protect her. To protect what they were building. And himself, if he could at least be honest with himself about that.

She melted against him for a moment before pulling back. "Who was that man who just left? Mitchell said you had a visitor."

"It was a small matter of business. Nothing important." That certainly wasn't the truth and he hated himself even more for it.

Diana's brow furrowed slightly. "At this hour? It's barely past nine."

"I was awake anyway. Habit of my past trade." He could still feel the fear at Crane's mention of Diana. And what would happen if the properties didn't sell in time to issue him the funds?

"Graham, you're shaking." She stepped closer, a look of concern in her eyes. "What's wrong?"

"Nothing." The word came out harsh, desperate. He needed her, needed to know she was safe, needed to claim her and protect her, and reassure himself that she was still his. Because she was. She was his. Nothing else mattered but protecting her.

Before she could speak again, he crashed his mouth against hers, needing her kiss to calm himself down. Diana gasped against his lips, and he plunged his tongue into her mouth as he backed her against the door.

"Graham—" she tried to speak when he moved to her neck, but he cut her off with another punishing kiss.

His hands were already working the buttons on her dress, a couple falling to the floor in his haste until her dress was pooled around her feet. He was thankful she hadn't been wearing stays and she lifted her arms as he pulled her chemise over her head. He needed to feel her skin, needed to be with what was his, needed to drown out the voices in his head that told him that everything was going to come crashing down on him.

"I need you," he ground out against her throat, his voice raw. "Please tell me you want me."

"I want you," she moaned against his lips, her hands tangling in his hair as he lifted her against the door. He reached between them to free his cock, then lowered her onto his full length.

Diana cried out, her nails digging into his shoulders. He started at a fast, hard pace, driving into her with all the fear and guilt consuming him. Needing to claim her and to know that all would work out.

"Mine," he growled against her ear. "You're mine. Nothing or no one shall ever take you from me."

"Never," Diana said, clinging tighter to him. "Graham...oh God—"

All of the emotion he was feeling was far too close to the

surface. He slowed his pace, taking her in long, slow movements pushing her harder against the door, his lips crashing down on hers again. His hand shifted between circling the sensitive flesh at her opening. He needed her to make her come, to feel her come undone in his arms.

Her core tightened around him so hard that he thought he might lose the ability to see. When she climaxed, moaning his name, Graham followed immediately, burying himself as deep as he could inside of her when he released.

They stayed pressed against the door, both breathing hard. Graham's face was buried in her neck, not wanting to let her go.

"Graham?" Diana's voice was soft, worried. Her fingers stroked through his hair. "Is something the matter?

"No." He pulled back, not meeting her eyes as he set her down and picked up her dress. "I just… needed you."

She caught his face in her hands, forcing him to look at her. "You should already know that you can tell me anything."

"I know," he said, helping her to get back into her dress.

"Then why won't you just tell me what it is? I can't help but feel like you are holding something back. And you had an odd reaction about that property."

He turned her so that he could fasten the buttons on her gown. "I just don't relish my lack of knowledge on such matters."

Graham silently cursed himself for being the biggest arse in all of England. It wasn't a lie, but it wasn't exactly the truth. And he'd been telling far too many half-truths as of late.

She spun back to face him and cupped his face in her hands. "That's what a partnership is. We help each other."

He knew he should just come clean. But the thought of Rothwell's vile offer made him see red all over again. And he'd protect her from the fear of something he'd never allow to occur.

"And we are partners. All is well," He kissed her more gently this time, trying to erase the worry from her eyes. "I'm sorry if I was too rough—"

"You weren't," she said, grinning at him and then moving

toward the desk, she started looking over some of the papers there. "But I still feel like there's something…whatever had consumed you in that manner. Not that I am complaining, I suppose."

He'd long missed his opportunity to explain by not telling her the moment they had become betrothed. He'd been mistaken in how he'd bungled the whole thing, and now no one would believe the truth. Trapping her into their marriage had never been his intention. That was most certainly fate that had put this beautiful woman in his life. And he didn't deserve her.

And if her family knew what Rothwell wanted, they would just as soon see him dead along with Rothwell. But he would keep her safe. Whatever the cost. He'd ensure Rothwell never laid eyes on her if he could help it.

Her fingers brushed over the ledgers and then a few pieces of parchment and she was becoming dangerously close to the first correspondence he'd received from Rothwell. "What is this correspondence? Does it pertain to the estates."

Panic set in as he realized that everything was left there on the desk. If she read any closer she would know what he was about, and everything would crumble down around him. He reached for her hand and pulled her to him, hugging her close. "I truly can't quite believe you're mine. I don't ever want to lose you."

And that was the complete truth.

"You aren't going to lose me," she replied, and then her lips curved into the most adorable grin. "Because you are also mine."

He placed a tender kiss on her brow. "There isn't a truer statement to be told."

I love you. The words were on the tip of his tongue. He felt them and he wanted to say them. He wanted to tell her how from the moment he kissed her in that gazebo that she was it for him. But no matter how much he willed himself to just speak the three simple, short words. He couldn't.

Not because he didn't mean it. But not until the matter was

resolved and he could come clean about all of it. He had decided. As soon as Rothwell was paid, he'd tell her everything.

CHAPTER TWELVE

Diana

One week later

DIANA SAT AT the writing desk in her parlor morning room, attempting to focus on her correspondence. She hadn't written a single letter in the time she'd become the Countess of Powis. Her husband kept her too preoccupied to have the energy to give it much thought. And every time she attempted to write, her thoughts would drift back to Graham and his behavior over the past several days.

He'd been affectionate and attentive, even more so as the days went on. He was even desperate at times in the way he'd take her. And as much as she adored the riding lessons and the physical attention, and the multiple orgasms, she couldn't help but wonder why.

And then there was that man she had seen leaving Graham's study. She didn't get a good look at him, but he appeared to have been rubbing his jaw. As if he were struck.

But what reason would her husband have to strike a man? The idea seemed impossible, but the way he'd taken her against the door was almost feral. And his hand was bruised.

Later, Diana went back to his study to get a look at the papers on his desk, but they weren't there. She searched through all of his drawers but didn't find the one that had mentioned something about a payment. And she questioned if she was even certain of what she saw. It was only a quick glimpse, so she could have misread the whole matter.

But anytime she asked if they might start implementing her ideas for the estates, she would very soon find herself in the afterglow of passion. He'd suggested that they take a couple weeks to just be a married couple before their lives became focused on their household matters. A small honeymoon of sorts, he'd said.

Diana wanted to believe that. She wanted to believe that it was all it was, a considerate husband wanting to shower her with affection. But deep down, her practical mind believed something was amiss. And the last time she'd ignored her practical mind, she had ended up betrothed to a stranger.

While that had worked out seemingly well, she wasn't certain she could ignore that voice inside of her again.

She only had time to ponder all of it at present because Graham had left for a meeting with his solicitor. She had half a mind to have Luna saddled and go for a ride in the park alone to clear her head. Her lessons had progressed and they had taken to riding in the park together, which was one of her favorite parts of the day.

The door opened and Hannah swept in, followed closely by Marina and Juliana.

"Mitchell allowed us to come up to surprise you. We've come to see how you are with our own eyes," Hannah announced, settling onto the sofa. "We've hardly seen you since the wedding."

"I am glad to see you all." Diana set down her pen. "I suppose I have been rather… occupied."

Marina's knowing look made Diana look away to avoid acknowledging her meaning. "Yes, we can imagine that your husband is taking up much of your time as you continue to learn all you can about each other."

"Indeed," Diana said, giving Marina a pointed look before motioning for them to take their seats in the nearby settee and chairs. "I am so fortunate that you all have called while he is out."

"And how are you finding married life?" Juliana asked gently. "You look radiant, and perhaps a bit tired."

Her friends were going to be relentless in teasing her.

"Marriage does change many things. I underestimated how much different my life would be." Diana reached for the bell pull to ring for tea. "It's all a bit overwhelming at times."

"Overwhelming?" Hannah leaned forward with concern. "In what way?"

Diana hesitated, twisting her wedding ring. She wanted to confide in them, but how could she voice her fears without sounding foolish? "It's just... everything happened so fast. I have learned things about my body I never knew. Thanks to Graham, I have become proficient on a horse, which is something I never thought I'd be able to do. And I share my life with someone I have come to care about, but still don't fully know."

"That's perfectly natural," Juliana said in support. "Marriage is a great adjustment, even under the best circumstances."

"But you do care for him?" Hannah asked.

Diana felt her skin grow warm. "Yes, I do. Very much so and more than I expected to. But that makes it all the more frustrating when I can't help but feel that he is hiding things from me."

"What makes you think he's hiding something?" Marina asked, already condemning the man given her tone.

"Well..." Diana glanced around at the expectant faces of her closest friends as she tried to decide what she would divulge. And then she finally decided she would tell them. "He asked for my help with estate management before we married. Said he had use for my knowledge and wanted me as a true partner in how things were managed. But now whenever I try to discuss improvements or ask about accounts, he brushes me off."

"All men think they know better about business," Marina said, rolling her eyes.

"But that's not it," Diana insisted. "He doesn't act superior. He acts... evasive. And there are other things that concern me."

There was a knock at the door and then a maid entered to

deliver the tea tray. Diana busied herself with preparing tea while her friends eagerly waited for her to continue.

"What other things?" Hannah asked once the servant had departed.

Diana set down the teapot and looked at each of her friends. "Days ago, I saw a man leaving Graham's study. I didn't get a good look at him, but something about him seemed… off. Not the sort of character that one would typically associate with. And he appeared to be holding his jaw, as if he'd been struck."

"Struck?" Juliana's eyes widened. "And you think—"

"I don't know what to think. When I found Graham afterward, his knuckles were bruised and he seemed off."

"That does sound concerning," Hannah said carefully. "Did you ask him about it?"

"Of course I did. But he dismissed it, saying it was nothing important. Then he…" Diana paused, not making eye contact with her friends. "Well, things became quite intense."

Marina's eyebrows rose knowingly. "Ah. And you let him distract you?"

"I couldn't seem to help myself," Diana admitted. "I have become nothing but a wanton where my husband is concerned, and I lose all sense. It's maddening."

"Is there anything else that concerns you about his behavior as of late?" Juliana asked.

Diana released a long audible breath. "I can't be certain, but I thought I saw some sort of demand to pay. I didn't see the amount, but it struck me as odd. And when I went to find the correspondence later, it was gone."

Marina huffed and then set her teacup down on the table. "Diana, I hate to ask this, but I feel I must. Are you absolutely certain Graham's intentions toward you were honorable from the beginning? I know you don't believe it to be the case, but it isn't a new tactic for a man to trap a woman."

Diana gulped, not ready to face what it would mean if Marina were right.

"I just can't believe that he would have done so." She wasn't certain her voice held the same conviction as her words.

"Of any of us, you are the one to think the most practically," Marina said, her voice gentle but relentless. "You were compromised quite conveniently for a man who had just inherited a title and it seems very well might have required funds. Now he's having mysterious meetings with unsavory characters, hiding financial documents, using physical intimacy to distract you from asking questions…"

"Marina!" Juliana protested.

"No, she's right to voice it," Diana said quietly, not wanting to believe any of it, but struggling to find another explanation. "I've wondered the same thing myself. And now he won't let me see the very finances I'm supposed to be helping with."

"But he gave you Luna," Hannah said, trying to offer comfort. "And he teaches you to ride every day. Surely that shows he cares about you, regardless?"

And that was the problem. He did seem as if he cared about her a great deal. But then why was he acting so strangely? And if he had trapped her and lied to her about it, couldn't he be capable of lying about other things? It could be the work of a fantastic actor.

"Perhaps," Diana said, still pondering.

"Have you demanded honesty from him?" Marina asked. "And refusing his… distractions until he explains whatever is going on?"

"I've tried," Diana said miserably. "But when he touches me, I become completely senseless. My resolve crumbles entirely and in those moments, none of it seems to matter."

"There seems to be much about marriage I don't understand," Hannah said, sipping her tea. "When the timing is better, I am going to need you to explain it to me."

Diana couldn't help but laugh a bit at that. "I promise I shall do so." Then her shoulders dropped. "Once I sort out what all of this means."

Before anyone could say anything else, the door opened and Graham swept in. "Diana, I... Oh, I didn't realize that you had company."

He gave a small bow. "Ladies, I apologize for interrupting."

"Not at all," Juliana said, rising from her chair. "We were just leaving, weren't we?"

Hannah squeezed her hand as she passed, whispering to her, "Guard your heart, dearest."

Her friends each gave him a small nod and took their leave without another word. Once they were alone, Graham moved to her side, his hand finding the small of her back in a way that had become like second nature for them.

"You appear upset," he said gently. "Were they troubling you about something?"

"No," Diana replied, turning to face him fully. "They're concerned about me."

"Why?" He stared back at her, the concern and care present in his expression. She just couldn't believe that it wasn't real.

Diana looked into his green eyes and she would swear that she spotted love reflected back in them.

"Because my husband is clearly distressed about something and is keeping things from me."

Graham's jaw tightened and then he reached for her. "Diana—"

"Don't," she said, stepping away from his touch. "Don't attempt to lull me into dropping this. Just... please. Tell me the truth."

For a moment, she thought he would finally tell her. His eyes were wild with emotion, his hands clenching and unclenching at his sides as if he were fighting some internal battle.

He raked his fingers through his hair. It was what he did every single time she questioned him. "I don't know what you want me to say."

She closed her eyes to gather her strength and then asked the burning question. "Did you trap me into marriage with you?"

His eyes went wide. "What?"

"Did you set up what occurred so I'd have to marry you?"

"No, Diana," he said quickly. "I swear to you that I didn't do so. You must believe me."

Fool as she was, she was inclined to believe him, but that still didn't explain some of his behavior.

"Do you need my dowry to pay off debts?"

He ran his hand down his face. "No. I do not. Your dowry is in an account that is meant for you and our future children."

She released a small sigh, relieved that the worst of her suspicions weren't true. If what he said was to be believed. But it still didn't explain why he had acted so strangely. And she decided she had to continue with her questions. "What about that man? Your hand was bruised. Did you strike him?"

Graham paced a couple steps before her, almost like a caged animal. "He was a shady character my cousin associated with. He is vile and I wanted him out of our home. I don't want someone like that anywhere near you."

She moved closer, searching his face desperately. "Then what is it that is troubling you? Why won't you just tell me."

Graham cupped her face in his hands, his touch so warm and gentle, that she wanted nothing more than to just lean into him and feel the hardness of his muscular chest. "Because you're everything to me, and I need to protect you."

"From what?"

Instead of answering, he kissed her, and Diana melted. She wanted to resist, to demand answers, but her treacherous body responded as it always did, wanting more and more of him.

When he pulled back, his eyes didn't leave hers. "Marrying you has been the best thing to ever happen to me. I did not plan it, and if the rules of our world were different, I would never have forced you to marry me, but I thank the stars every night that we have found each other. Just please believe that."

He kissed her again, deeper this time, and Diana let him because she did believe him. Even if that meant ignoring her practical mind once again.

CHAPTER THIRTEEN

Graham

"THIRTY-FIVE THOUSAND POUNDS." Graham's solicitor, Henry Foulis, slid the bank draft across his desk. "The Somerset property has closed. Want me to have this deposited to your account?"

Graham stared at the number on the draft, not bothering to hide his disappointment. Diana had valued it at forty thousand minimum. "That's all?"

"The buyer was quite firm, my lord. Given the urgency of your sale—"

"They exploited the opportunity." Graham tucked the draft into his chest pocket. He'd wanted to order the draft for Rothwell himself and not involve his solicitor, so he might as well take the drafts. "And the Devon property?"

Foulis shifted in his chair. "Ah, yes. There has been…a delay."

That could not happen. Rothwell expected payment in a matter of days. "What do you mean by a delay?"

"An issue with the funds. The buyer's solicitor assures me that it will be settled and the property will still transfer ownership as planned. Eighty-five thousand pounds for that one."

The amount would hardly matter if Graham couldn't pay Rothwell by his deadline. Graham leaned forward, practically snarling, "How long?"

"They have requested another week."

Graham gripped the edge of the desk until his knuckles went white. "That's not possible. The sale must close today."

"My lord, I understand your urgency, but—"

"You understand nothing." Graham shot to his feet, sending Foulis's inkwell rolling. "Do we have any other buyers?"

The solicitor's face flushed. "That would close today? That is just not possible. You are better off waiting for this matter to settle."

But he didn't have the time to wait. Diana's safety depended on it. He wasn't certain what he would do, but there had to be something. He was now ten thousand pounds short. But it might as well be one hundred thousand without the sale of the other property. With less than one thousand pounds remaining in his account, he had nothing else.

"Send for me immediately if we hear words of the funds," Graham commanded and rose from his chair. "And press for the payment to be given."

He took his leave, slamming the door behind him. Ten thousand pounds. How in the world was he going to come up with ten thousand pounds?

Graham dismissed his carriage, deciding that the walk would better serve him. He racked his brain thinking of anything that he could. Did he have anything else that he could sell quickly?

The bank was just ahead of him and he stopped and leaned against the brick wall of one of the shops, taking his head in his hands. What in the devil was he going to do? There was the account with Diana's dowry, but he couldn't use those funds. He had to come up with something else.

He groaned.

"Something troubling you?"

Graham looked up to see the bastard himself, Rothwell, standing before him.

"Nothing that concerns you." Graham straightened, fighting the urge to plant his fist in the man's smug face. Again. The bruising from where he hit the man before was still barely visible.

"Oh, but everything concerns me until I receive my payment." Rothwell's smile was cold. "You look rather... distressed. Surely your plans to raise my funds are going well?"

Graham said nothing, but Rothwell chuckled as he brushed something off of his shoulder. *Of all people to run into on the street, it has to be that blackguard.* He started to walk away before he caused a scene.

"Difficulties, perhaps?" Rothwell called out to him, louder than Graham would have liked. "I suppose we could discuss alternative arrangements."

Graham spun on his heel and came nose to nose with the man. "There will be no alternative arrangements. You'll have your money."

"When?"

"When it is due." He still wasn't sure how he was going to accomplish that, but he still had a couple days and he was going to need them if he had any chance. *Or to take Diana and run.* Because that option was becoming far more likely with every minute that passed.

"I don't think you have the funds. But I'm certain your wife would be far more effective than you with her connections. I'm certain you gained access to a dowry and funds settled on her." Rothwell challenged. "Perhaps I should call on your pretty little wife and discuss the matter with her."

Graham shoved the man into the alley and pinned him against the brick wall. "You won't go anywhere near her."

"You are of the mind that you have the upper hand here, Powis."

"What's to stop me from ending you right here and now?" Graham growled, pushing his forearm tighter into the man's neck. He had never punched anyone before Rothwell, but he would do a great many things if it meant Diana remained safe.

Rothwell laughed, between choking for air. "You're stupider than you appear."

Graham loosened his hold on the man's neck, but still kept him against the wall. "How do you figure that?"

"Do you think this ends if I disappear? I have men that will make sure you pay. And they won't practice the same restraint as me when it comes to making you suffer through using your new wife's body to make their point."

Graham cut off the man's breath again. He could hardly see through his rage. "Do not mention my wife again."

Rothwell shoved him back and fought to catch his breath. Then he started laughing again. "The offer still stands if you want her to earn five thousand pounds on her back. And her knees, and stomach. But since you can't keep your hands to yourself, my men get a turn, too."

Unable to stop himself, Graham unleashed punch after punch into the man's face. Rothwell fought back, shoving Graham back against the wall, pinning him so that he couldn't move and then snarled in his face. "You're going to regret that. Now get me my money. And if you think to try to run. We'll find you both."

Graham heaved and he knew what he had to do. This wouldn't end until he had paid Rothwell. He'd get him the funds and then he and Diana would go to the country for a while so Rothwell could move on to harass someone else. And he could hire guards to ensure Diana remained safe until he could be certain the threat had passed.

"I have your money," Graham seethed. "Wait here and I will bring you the bank draft."

Rothwell released him and stepped back, giving him a satis-fied grin. "There. Was that so difficult? I knew you would see things my way."

Graham lumbered away from the alley and composed himself just before he stepped back onto the main street. He was thankful he had been wearing gloves, but his fist throbbed.

He had no choice in what he was about to do. Diana wouldn't be safe until Rothwell was paid. The blackguard was a low life who wouldn't cease in making their lives miserable until he had his money.

He only had one option to get Rothwell what he wanted.

Diana's dowry.

The thought of using even a single pound of the money from her dowry made him want to cast up his accounts. He'd told her he didn't need her dowry to pay any debts. And he had meant it at the time. If that second property would have sold in enough time, it wouldn't have come to this. But he can't risk Rothwell getting the mind to corner her.

It would just be ten thousand pounds, and he'd return it as soon as he had the proceeds from the Devon property.

His hands shook as he walked toward the bank, each step feeling like it was a step closer to losing Diana. By the time he reached the bank his nerves were shot. If he thought he had any other way, he would take it.

He left with the bank draft for Rothwell and returned to the alley as quickly as he could so he could be done with the mess.

Rothwell was exactly where Graham had left him, examining his fingernails with his bruised and bloodied face.

"Forty-five thousand pounds," Graham said, throwing the bank draft at the man's feet. "We're finished."

Rothwell bent to retrieve the draft, pleased with himself. "Well, well. See what a man can accomplish when he puts his mind to it."

"It's done. Stay away from my wife."

"You don't think she might like to know what her husband has been up to?" Rothwell tucked the draft into his waistcoat. "And you bloodied my face, and expect I should just let that go?"

Graham stepped forward, clenching his fists. "If you go near her—"

"You'll what?" Rothwell straightened his coat, seemingly unconcerned by Graham's threat.

Graham drew a deep breath and raised his hands to indicate he wouldn't attack him again. "You have your money. Our business is done."

"As long as you stay out of my way." Rothwell said, turning to walk the other way, but then turned back for one last taunt. "Do give my regards to the lovely Lady Powis."

Graham stood alone in the filthy alley, wondering what he would say or do next. Nausea swept over him as he thought about facing Diana.

He'd stolen from money promised to his wife. And betrayed her trust. Arguably he had been doing that for the past few weeks.

When he finally reached their townhouse after roaming the streets on his long walk home, he heard women's voices coming from the drawing room. Diana's bright laughter made the guilt twist through his body.

He crept to their bed chamber and let Baker help to right his appearance. Baker eyed him curiously as he tended to his hand and then he donned a fresh pair of gloves.

But he couldn't put off facing his wife anymore. He descended the stairs and made his way to the drawing room.

"Graham!" Diana exclaimed as soon as he appeared in the doorway, her face lighting up when she saw him. "Perfect timing. Look who has arrived!"

He glanced over Diana's shoulder and saw his mother coming to a stand and approaching with her arms extended. "My son."

He was glad to see his mother, but the timing couldn't have been worse. "Mother. What a wonderful surprise."

"I decided I simply couldn't wait any longer to meet my new daughter." Augusta's gaze never left his face, studying him. "I've been getting to know our Diana here. And you were right, I adore her very much."

"The feeling is mutual," Diana said, slipping her arm through his. Her kind touch was just another blow. "Though we are glad you have returned. Although, you look exhausted."

"Just a long day with my solicitor." Another half-truth. "And then I decided to walk, and it ended up being quite long."

"Well, you're home now." Diana rose on her toes to kiss his

cheek, and Graham closed his eyes as he hated himself more and more. "Your mother was just telling me about your childhood. Apparently, you once tried to convince your governess that Latin was optional because horses don't speak it."

"I was eight," Graham protested weakly.

"You were incorrigible," Augusta said with a strained smile. "Diana, dear, would you mind checking on our tea? I'd like a moment to catch up with my son properly."

"Of course." Diana squeezed Graham's arm. "She promised to tell me more stories of little Graham over supper."

The moment Diana left the room, Augusta gripped his arms forcing him to focus on her.

"What is the matter?"

Graham tried to pull away, but his mother wouldn't relinquish her hold. "Nothing, Mother. I'm fine."

"I raised you, Graham Clive. I know when you are feeling guilty about something." Augusta's voice was barely above a whisper. "Tell me. Now. If you have been out there making a fool of that kind, beautiful girl, I am going to take a horse whip to you."

He couldn't let his mother believe that he was capable of such a horrid thing. There wasn't anything in the world that could make him be unfaithful to Diana. "I had to pay off the gambling debts that the previous Powis left. And…"

"And what? Surely it can't be all that bad."

"I had to use some of the funds allocated to Diana. Without her knowledge." Speaking the words and confessing to his mother didn't ease any of his guilt.

Augusta's frown deepened. "Then you have to tell her."

Graham ran both hands down his face. "I can't, Mother. It's just temporary. I have a property up for sale and as soon as I get the money, I'm going to replace it. She'll never know. And then it will be like it never happened."

The slap came swift and sharp, echoing in the quiet room.

Graham touched his stinging cheek, too stunned to speak.

"You fool," Augusta hissed, her eyes filling with tears. "That's how it starts. You keep certain things from your wife and then it becomes far too easy to keep more. Where does it end?"

"It's not like that, Mother," Graham said, still in disbelief that his mother slapped him. "I accidentally compromised Diana. Her father and brother already don't trust me."

"Of course they don't trust you. You lied to them. You are still lying to them."

Wasn't his mother supposed to be on his side and support him? If one person might understand, wasn't it supposed to be his mother? "I thought I could handle the situation and was doing what was best. If they knew about this whole mess, they might encourage her to leave. Or see me on the dueling ground. I know it's a mess, but I love her, Mother. And I can't lose her. I had no choice."

"There's always a choice. You could have told Diana the truth. Asked for her help. Trusted your wife and what you are building together." Augusta moved to the window, her back rigid. "Instead, you've become exactly what you tried to prevent—a fortune hunter who married for money to solve his problems."

"That's not what happened."

"I know my son, and I know that's not what happened. But I am not the one you need to convince. And you shall only do so by being honest."

Before Graham could answer, Diana returned with a tea tray, her smile falling when she saw them.

"Is everything all right? You both look rather serious."

"Just catching up on a few things," Augusta said, her voice calm.

Diana set down the tray and looked between them with concern. "Nothing troubling, I hope?"

"Nothing you need worry about, sweetheart," Graham said, the lie burning his throat. "Mother was just concerned that I might be in need of rest."

"Well, she's not wrong. You seem exhausted." Diana moved to pour tea, and Graham watched her, hoping that he hadn't ruined everything.

"Your mother's been telling me we should take a proper honeymoon," Diana continued, handing him a cup. "Get away from London for a while. What do you think?"

His chest tightened. "That sounds wonderful."

And he meant it. It did sound like the most wonderful thing he'd heard all day.

"I was thinking we could visit our estates. I'm so eager to see them and confirm the strategy for the improvements we discussed." Diana's eyes sparkled with enthusiasm. "And I'd like to visit with the estate managers if you would let me."

"Anything you'd like," Graham said, forcing a smile.

Dinner passed with Graham saying very little. He watched Diana chat with his mother, making plans for the future, and discussing every topic under the sun. He never deserved her, but he still wanted her more than anything.

After supper, they retired to their chamber for the evening. He undressed and climbed into their bed while Diana was in the adjoining room having Mary help with her evening ablutions. He stared at the canopy wondering what he should do. How could he ensure he didn't lose her, but that he could look in the mirror without hating himself?

Diana blew out the candle on the bedside table and crawled into bed with him, nestling into his side.

"You were quiet tonight," Diana said, tracing the lines on his chest with her finger.

"Just tired." And full of self-loathing.

"Poor darling." She leaned closer, and placed a sweet kiss on his cheek. "You need some rest. Perhaps don't send your carriage away again."

She was so kind and thoughtful. And he didn't deserve any of it. He should tell her everything. Including that he was completely and wholly in love with her.

"Diana, I—"

"What is it?" Her sapphire eyes searched his face.

"You're everything to me," he said instead, the coward's version of truth. But if he could just get the funds back in the account. Then he could at least prove that he had never intended for things to occur the way that they did. He had to give himself the best chance. Even if that made him a fool.

She nuzzled her nose into his neck. "I feel the same."

His arms tightened around her. One week. Just one more week until the Devon property closed and he could replace the money.

One week to live this deception.

One week before his world was righted or it all came crashing down.

CHAPTER FOURTEEN
Diana

DIANA ADJUSTED HER gloves as she stepped out of the carriage onto Bond Street, grateful for the crisp morning air while she left Graham at home to spend some time with his mother. Lydia followed, then Hannah and Marina, to browse a few shops. She hadn't had a shopping trip with her friends since she married.

"The modiste first," Marina declared. "I would like to find a new pair of gloves for the next ball."

"And I need ribbon," Hannah added. "The blue silk at Madame's would be perfect."

Diana enjoyed the opportunity to spend a bit of time with her friends, though her mind kept drifting to Graham. He'd come home exhausted last night. And it had been the first night of their marriage that they hadn't been intimate before bed.

"Diana, you're wool-gathering," Lydia said gently, linking their arms. "Are you feeling all right?"

"Yes, of course." Diana forced a jovial tone.

"We have missed having you at the balls with us," Hannah said from behind her.

Diana surprisingly hadn't missed attending such events at all. "After the gossip surrounding our marriage, we are enjoying this time together. We are planning to depart for a honeymoon soon to tour our estates."

"So things are going well then?" Marina asked, an edge to her question.

"Yes," Diana replied, but she wasn't certain it was the truth. She had been satisfied with the answers from Graham after she'd questioned him, but something still didn't seem quite right.

"Lady Powis."

There was a man standing before her. He was in his thirties with dark hair and eyes that didn't quite match his pleasant smile. Something about him made her uncomfortable, particularly the bruising all over his face and nose.

"I don't believe we've been introduced," she said carefully.

"Forgive me. Silas Rothwell, at your service." He bowed elegantly. "I'm an associate of your husband's."

Associate? She had never heard the man's name before. But he appeared somewhat familiar to her.

"I see," Diana said, attempting to move past him, but he shifted slightly, blocking her path.

"Indeed. Your husband and I just concluded some rather significant business yesterday. Quite profitable for both of us, I'd say."

Lydia, Marina, and Hannah, stepped closer to Diana, as if they were protecting her.

"Is everything all right, Diana?" Marina asked.

"Perfectly," Diana said, raising her chin. "Mr. Rothwell was just leaving."

"Not quite yet." Rothwell's smile widened, and she stared at the bruising on his jaw. Could it be the same man she had seen leaving their home? "I simply wanted to congratulate you on your marriage. Your husband is a fortunate man."

"Thank you," Diana said stiffly.

"Very fortunate for Powis, indeed." Rothwell pretended to examine his gloves. "Your dowry was particularly helpful in settling certain… obligations."

Diana wobbled a bit, but Hannah gripped her arm. "I beg your pardon?"

"Oh dear, did he not tell you?" Rothwell's eyes lit up. "Your husband owed me quite a substantial sum. Well, his cousin did, but debts pass with titles, don't they? Powis was quite creative in gathering the funds through property sales and I suspect your dowry contribution. But you will be glad to know what he has paid in full."

"You're lying." The words came out as a whisper.

"Am I? Why don't you ask him? And when you do, be sure to tell him that he should be more careful when he decides to strike a man."

Diana's vision blurred. She heard Marina's sharp intake of breath before she threatened the man if he didn't get away from them.

"Diana," Lydia said sternly. "We should go."

She climbed back into the carriage and fell into the seat, her heart shattering in her chest and she replayed everything in her head.

As soon as Marina climbed in, she said across from her, "That vile man! How dare he approach you—"

"But was he telling the truth?" Diana's mouth went dry. "About the dowry?"

"We don't know that," Hannah said quickly. "He could be lying to cause trouble."

"But this would explain everything."

The ride home passed in tense silence. Diana's mind raced through every interaction with Graham over the past weeks. His refusal to show her the household accounts. The way he'd deflect her questions with intimacy. The papers she'd glimpsed on his desk about payments.

And then if used the funds that he told her was allocated for her and their future children, he had looked her in the eye and lied.

By the time they reached the townhouse, Diana was shaking with rage.

"Perhaps we should—"

"Just go," Diana said, after a footman handed her down from the carriage. "I'll be all right."

She didn't believe those words, but she didn't need her friends to help her face Graham. It was something she had to do on her own.

Once Diana was inside, she tossed her reticule and hat aside. She immediately went to Graham's study, and found it empty.

She went to his desk, trying each drawer. The bottom one was locked. She took a letter opener from his desk and worked the lock. The wood splinters from where she forced the lock open, but she was able to access the drawer.

Part of her felt guilty about breaking into his locked drawer. But she had to know if he was lying to her. It might contain the only proof to the contrary so she could confirm that she could trust him and the man was nothing but a liar.

Inside the drawer were bank statements, correspondence, and property deeds. She spread them across the desk and began to read through each of the papers.

Then her eyes landed on a withdrawal slip dated yesterday. Ten thousand pounds from her dowry account, that had been transferred to another account. And then another slip for a forty-five-thousand-pound bank draft that has been drawn up.

Next was correspondence from Rothwell demanding that he be paid the funds that he was owed. And then property sale documents and the ledgers for a couple of the estates with the parchment where she'd written the valuation and the plans for the enhancements.

She thought back on their conversation. The way that he'd asked her questions about the value of the properties and how he never wanted to discuss the estates after that. She had solved his problem for him. Told him exactly which properties to sell without knowing about it. He'd used her while lying to her face.

And if he could lie to her and keep all of this from her, what else was he capable of? She thought she knew him, loved him even. But he was as much of a stranger to her as the day they'd met.

"Diana?"

Graham appeared in the doorway, appearing confused. Was everything a performance?

"What are you doing? I didn't realize you were home. Mother would love for you to join us for tea. I think she adores you more than me."

Tears welled in the corners of Diana's eyes. She loved the man before her, and he betrayed her. She had been the worst kind of fool to let him have her heart.

Graham rushed to her. "What is the matter?"

She pushed him back, too afraid to allow herself to be in his arms. Because as angry as she was, she still wanted him to hold her. Which was why she couldn't trust herself.

He glanced at the desk and the color drained from his face. "Diana. Please, you have to let me explain."

"Explain how you lied to me? How you used my dowry after you said you wouldn't. You've been hiding things from me from the start. And I let you trap me so you could have it all. You got my body, my knowledge, and my dowry."

Graham reached for her again, but she stepped back. "Diana, I swear to you that what happened in the garden wasn't some kind of plan. You must believe me. I will tell you everything like I should have from the start."

Diana shook her head, not wanting to hear anymore. Because she didn't trust herself not to believe him. She took off from the study and raced toward the staircase in the foyer.

"Diana," Graham called after her.

"Where is he?" A familiar voice boomed from the front doorway.

Elias.

"Brother," Diana cried and ran in front of him. "Please. Don't make matters worse."

"Trust me, sister. This will be much better after I have dealt with the bastard."

Graham appeared in the foyer, holding his hands up. "Elias, please, allow me to explain—"

"Explain?" Elias released Diana and stalked toward Graham. "Explain how you lied and tricked my sister from the start so you could steal from her?"

"What is all this commotion?" Augusta appeared at the top of the stairs, looking between them with alarm.

"Mother, please just go back to your room," Graham said quickly.

"I will do no such thing." Augusta descended the staircase and moved to stand by her son. "What has happened?"

"Your son is a liar and thief," Elias spat. "He took ten thousand pounds from Diana's dowry to pay gambling debts."

There was a knock at the front door, and when Mitchell opened it, Lydia entered, followed by Marina and Hannah, with Hudson and Matt close behind.

"I had to tell Elias," Lydia said quietly to Diana. "You shouldn't face this matter alone."

"Why are Hudson and Matt here?" Diana asked, mortified that most of her friends were witnessing the most embarrassing and devastating moment of her life while her heart was broken wide open.

"They were with Elias, and we all couldn't keep up with him when he tore out of the house," Hannah said.

Diana watched Elias take a couple steps closer to Graham, nostrils flaring. "I don't require any assistance in this matter. He's a lowlife who took advantage of my sister so he could get his hands on her dowry, just as I knew he did all along. You really almost had us all fooled."

"That's not what happened," Matt said, stepping to join Graham's side.

"You mean to tell me you knew about this?" Elias thundered.

"Graham told me about the situation with Rothwell, yes," Matt replied calmly. "He was afraid to tell you because he thought you might react much like this."

Hudson stepped forward to join Elias. "You should have known that Wilton would align with a liar."

Diana watched the men square off with each other and she wasn't certain what to believe. He had still lied, misled, and used her. And for that, she wasn't certain he could be forgiven, even if Elias let him live.

"Rothwell was threatening you," Graham said desperately, focusing on Diana. "He said he'd hurt you, to do unspeakable things to you if I didn't pay—"

"Was that before or after you used my sister to save your own skin?"

"That's not what happened!" Graham ran both hands through his hair. "The compromise was an accident. I never planned—"

"I am done hearing your lies," Elias spat.

Matt stepped closer to Elias. "Come on Elias. "I know Graham. And he—"

"You vouched for him," Hudson rounded on Matt. "You brought him into our circle. And this is what he's done."

"The money will be replaced," Graham said frantically. "A property in Devon closes within a week."

Diana stepped between the men, done hearing them all bicker about her life. "But you lied to me, Graham. All you had to do was explain the situation to me. I would have believed you."

"Diana, please," Graham moved toward her, but Elias shoved him back.

"Don't you dare touch her."

"She's my wife!"

"Not for long," Elias snarled. "If there is any way to get her away from you, I am going to do it."

"Please," Graham said, his eyes locked on hers. "Diana, I love you. I should have told you so days ago. I know I've handled this terribly, but everything I did was because I love you and had to ensure you were safe."

She had longed to hear those words from him. Longed to

push aside those nagging feelings about what he was hiding and believe that he loved her as much as she loved him. But she couldn't be certain it wasn't more of his half-truths and lies.

"Love?" Diana laughed bitterly. "You don't know what love is. Love is trust. Love is honesty. Love is partnership. You gave me none of those things."

Augusta moved to Graham's side, placing a hand on his arm. "Graham, perhaps we should give Diana a bit of space."

She did need to remove herself from whatever this situation was. To have a moment to think without her brother and friends staring at her, expecting her to hate him as much as they did. When she didn't hate him. She couldn't. It would be far simpler if she were able to hate him.

Diana moved toward the stairs, but Graham clasped her hand.

"Diana, please. Just listen—"

"Let her go," Elias warned.

He did and when she looked back at Graham, the pain in his expression almost broke her. "I'm sorry, Diana."

But she wasn't ready to hear it. She hurried up the stairs until she reached her chamber, not the one they shared together, but the one that belonged to her. Diana locked the doors to keep anyone from entering. She didn't wish to see any of them.

Diana paced her chamber, wiping away the tears that she'd finally released. How could he have done this to her? He had given her a horse and showered her with affection. They'd spend almost every day together, and they had been the best days of her life.

But she couldn't decide to forgive him until she'd had time to think the matter through and approach it with a practical mind.

Diana looked in her mirror to see her puffy, red eyes. The heartbreak was written all over her face. She looked around the room, and the walls were closing in on her. She needed fresh air and to feel like she had a bit of control over her own future. Even if, as a woman, she had very little control and would either live with her husband or go back to her father.

She tried to think of what would calm her. What would help her get clarity and give her some sense of herself? And then she knew what she must do. She'd go for a ride. The wind in her hair, free from the confines of the house, would give her the clarity she needed to face the chaos of her life.

Diana quickly changed into her riding habit without help. As quietly as possible, she opened her bedroom door that led to the hallway. She looked both ways to ensure no one was there, but she could still hear the men arguing in the foyer.

She crept down the servant stairs and made her way to the stables. On the way out the door, she ran right into Mitchell. But she didn't stop. Mitchell would tell Graham where she went, but she would have enough of a head start that he couldn't stop her.

Once she reached the stables, she asked the first groom she saw to saddle her horse. She looked back towards the house, watching for Graham to come running after her.

A few moments later, the groom handed her the reins and helped her with the mounting block. Looking back towards the house once more, she was still in the clear. She flicked the reins and took off. She kept Luna at a walking pace all the way to the park.

Once she reached one of the grassy areas, she urged Luna into a canter. In a matter of moments, the tension had released from her shoulders and she was more comfortable in the saddle. This was exactly what she needed. A long ride with her horse and then she'd face whatever the future did or didn't hold with her husband.

She pushed Luna harder, needing the speed as if it would help her to outrun the pain. The mare responded eagerly, moving from canter to gallop along the park's path.

Briefly closing her eyes, she took a deep breath. Despite everything, she still loved him. And he said that he loved her.

She opened them as a stray dog was about to run across her path. Diana screamed and tried to slow Luna. She pulled the reins too hard and Luna stopped abruptly, lifting her front legs. The movement caused Diana to be thrown back off of the horse, her body slamming into the ground.

Then everything went dark.

CHAPTER FIFTEEN
Graham

GRAHAM STOOD FROZEN in the foyer, staring at the stairs where Diana had disappeared. His entire world had come crashing down around him, just as he feared. He had done everything wrong, except for loving Diana. He would never feel sorry for that.

"You should be horsewhipped," Elias snarled, shoving Graham hard enough that he stumbled back into the wall. He drew his fist back and planted a hard punch to Graham's cheek.

"Elias, enough," Matt said, stepping between them to push Elias back. "None of this helps."

Graham made no attempt to defend himself or fight back. That was a deserved facer from his wife's brother, to defend her honor. He regained his footing and drew a deep breath, his cheek throbbing.

"Won't it?" Hudson moved to stand beside Elias. "Because I think breaking his jaw might make me feel considerably better about what he did to our Diana."

Augusta placed herself firmly between her son and the angry men. "Gentlemen, this accomplishes nothing. Diana just needs time to clear her head and then sit down and talk all of this through."

"What she needs is to be free of this sham of a marriage,"

Elias spat.

"It's not a sham," Graham cried out, willing Elias to believe him. "I love her."

"You have a peculiar way of showing it," Marina said coldly from where she stood with Hannah and Lydia.

He opened his mouth to speak and then closed it again. There was no defense or justification for the poor decisions he'd made. He could have handled it all so differently. And now it might be too late.

Mitchell appeared in the foyer, and motioned for Graham. "My lord, Lady Powis has… that is, she's gone to the stables. She seemed rather upset."

Graham felt the blood rush to his ears. "What?"

"She passed me on her way out. I would have stopped her, but she seemed determined."

Graham was already moving toward the door, but Elias grabbed his arm. "Why would she be at the stables?"

"Because she's upset and she loves riding her horse." Graham wrenched free. "She's still learning, and must ensure—"

"You taught her to ride?" Elias exploded. "If something happens to her…"

Graham didn't wait to hear the rest. He ran for the mews, his heart pounding. She had become a proficient rider when he was with her, but anything could happen. When he got there, Luna and Diana were gone.

"Saddle Midnight," Graham commanded the groom. "Now."

He raced down the road, hoping to catch up with her as quickly as possible. She could continue to refuse to talk to him, but he had to ensure her safety. His wife had become a proficient rider, but many things could happen that she wasn't prepared to handle on her own. When he reached the park, he saw her in the distance. She had Luna in a canter.

Diana truly was the most beautiful woman that he had ever seen, and he ached at the thought of losing her love. If he wasn't so worried for her safety, he would be proud of how graceful she looked upon her beloved horse. He gave Midnight his head to catch up with her, then saw a stray dog running towards Diana's path. His heart stopped when he saw Luna kick up and Diana come crashing to the ground. "Diana!"

He reached her and leapt off of his horse, racing to her side and crouching beside her. "Diana sweetheart. Wake up, darling. Please."

She wasn't moving. Graham's entire body was shaking. He felt her neck, praying there was a pulse. He closed his eyes and released a large stream of air when he could make out a rhythm. "Diana. Please wake up." He looked around, trying to decide what to do.

"I've got you, sweetheart. You're going to be all right. I will make sure of it." Tears sprang from his eyes. He couldn't lose her. This was all his fault. He's the one who got her the horse. He's the one who broke her trust and her heart. If only he hadn't played the part of a coward.

Graham picked her up and cradled her against him, holding her steady with one arm. He grabbed the reins of both horses and guided them along with him. He'd hail a hackney to get her home to avoid jostling her more than necessary.

Graham walked as quickly as he could and got her into a hackney. He tied the horses to the back and gave the driver the address of his townhouse. When they arrived at their home, he cradled her in his arms again and jumped down from the carriage. "Wait here. My man will pay you handsomely and retrieve my horses."

He raced through the front door as quickly as he could without moving Diana too much. Mitchell appeared right away.

"Send for the doctor immediately. Tell him he must come straight away. Generously pay the hackney driver and have someone retrieve and stable our horses. Also, send Mary to our chamber."

Mitchell sprang into action to take care of all the Graham asked.

"What the hell happened?" Elias shouted. There were gasps and cries that rang out as everyone swarmed him from a nearby drawing room.

"She fell. Luna threw her." Graham couldn't let go of Diana even as Elias reached for her. "We need a physician. Now."

"Give her to me," Elias demanded.

"No." Graham's arms tightened around her. "I've got her."

Graham climbed the stairs, hugging Diana to him. He entered their shared chamber and pulled back the bedding to lay her down, resting her head on the pillows.

Mary entered the room and gasped. "What has happened, my lord?"

Graham fought the tears that were welled up in his eyes. "She took off riding on her own. I went after her and got there too late. She had a fall. Mitchell sent for the doctor. Help me get her changed out of her habit before the doctor arrives."

Mary and Graham removed Diana's habit and dressed her in a night rail. He pulled the covers up over her to keep her warm. He checked her pulse again and was relieved to find that it was still strong. Even in sleep, she was still breathtakingly beautiful, and it made every part of him ache with how much he longed for her to wake.

He laid his hand on her chest to feel the inhale and exhale of her breath to keep himself from losing his mind.

"Elias is enraged," his mother said, entering the chamber. "The only thing keeping him from coming up here is fear that fighting with you will worsen her condition. How is her breathing?"

Graham looked up at his mother. He couldn't speak and he could no longer hold back the tears. His legs gave out from underneath him, his knees hitting the floor. He folded his arms to prop himself on the side of her bed and released all of the pain from how he feared losing her.

Augusta rushed to her son's side. "Dearest, you must be strong for her. I know you are blaming yourself, but you didn't cause her to fall. Right now, the only thing that matters is taking care of Diana."

Graham raised his head and clasped his fingers around Diana's hand, wiping his eyes with his other hand. His mother brushed his hair from his face, like she did when he was a boy. Augusta walked to the other side of the bed and sat beside Diana, holding her other hand.

Mitchell appeared a few moments later and had the doctor with him.

The man entered the room and began assessing Diana and then immediately looked to Graham. "Please explain to me what has occurred in as much detail as possible."

Graham discussed the fall and detailed her positioning during the incident. He answered all the doctor's questions, not releasing his wife's hand for a single moment.

"I need to examine her now. Everyone must wait downstairs so I can concentrate and listen to her breathing and heart rate."

"I'm staying. I'm her husband." Graham stood to face the man.

"That is precisely why you need to wait downstairs, my lord. I need to focus, and you will demand immediate answers. I promise I will come to you directly after I have examined her. Her maid can stay with me for the examination."

Augusta crossed to the other side of the room and took her son's arm. "Let's go, son. Allow the doctor to work."

Graham let his mother lead him out of the room. They made their way to the drawing room where everyone waited. Matt leaned against the windowsill, watching outside the window. Augusta took a seat on the settee, rapping her fingers on the arm.

"The doctor is with her now. He will inform us as soon as he can," Graham said, not making eye contact with any of them.

He took to pacing the room, back and forth. No one spoke, only waited.

The tension in the room was palpable. It felt like hours before the doctor finally joined them. Lydia looped her arm through

Elias's, attempting to keep him calm. Everyone surrounded the doctor, remaining quiet to hear everything that he had to say.

Graham held his breath. Afraid to hear the words. Diana had to be all right. It was the only truth he would accept.

Because he couldn't live without her.

CHAPTER SIXTEEN
Graham

T HE DOCTOR STEPPED further into the room to speak to everyone. "Her ladyship is still unconscious. I don't see any breaks or bleeding concerns."

Elias jumped in. "When will she wake up?"

"Head injuries are tricky. She's stable, and I have every reason to believe that she will wake up soon, but we won't know for sure if there will be long-term damage until she wakes up. She will need someone to stay with her around the clock. Her maid is sitting with her now."

"Is there anything we can do? Can we give her anything?" Hannah spoke this time.

"Right now, all we can do is wait. Send for me as soon as she awakens or if there are any changes, and I will do another exam."

"Thank you. We appreciate your help," Lydia said, clutching her husband's arm.

The doctor bowed to the room and left them all to process what was shared. The silence in the room was brief before Elias turned back to Graham. "This is all your fault. If you hadn't given her that damn horse." The fury in his eyes turned to sadness, and Elias covered his face with his hands.

Lydia joined his side. "My love, this is no one's fault. We need to pull together for Diana right now. She needs all of us."

Graham stumbled as his legs threatened to give out. Augusta crossed the distance and steadied her son. "It'll be all right." She brushed the hair from his face and gave him a solemn smile.

"You can't possibly know that!" Elias snapped, then he hung his head. "My apologies."

"None needed, my lord. These are trying circumstances. I adore my new daughter so very much." Augusta smiled and stepped towards Elias, taking his hand in hers. "I believe she also has your passionate spirit."

Tears formed in Elias's eyes. He pulled Augusta's hand to his lips, but didn't speak.

Once Elias released her hand, Augusta addressed the room. "Who wishes to stay tonight? I will have the staff ensure we have rooms ready and ensure that Cook is prepared to accommodate everyone."

"I believe we all will stay," Hannah said to Augusta.

Graham went to depart from the room. "I'm going to see my wife. My mother will ensure you all have anything you need until I return."

Elias stopped him. "I'm going with you."

Graham turned to face Elias. He stood the tallest and most sure of himself that he'd been since Diana's accident. "Whatever issues you have with me. You will leave them in this room. My wife doesn't need any of this in her presence while she is fighting to come back to us. If you cannot comply, I will have you removed."

Elias sneered, but nodded in agreement. "Very well. Elias and I will sit with Diana first and trade off with the rest of you. I am sure you all wish to see her." There were nods around the room.

Graham turned to exit the room, not looking back to see if Elias followed. The gentlemen reached Diana's chamber and quietly opened the door. Mary had placed a chair by the bed, which she sat in, while she held Diana's hand.

"Mary, why don't you take a break? Her ladyship's brother and I intend to sit with her for a while."

Mary nodded, wiping a tear from her face. She closed the door behind her.

Graham motioned for Elias to take the chair next to the bed. He did so and took his sister's hand. Graham walked to the other side of the bed and sat next to her, taking her other hand. "You have a house full of people here who love you and are ready for you to come back to us." He drew her hand to his lips, a couple of tears falling from his eyes.

Elias watched him, not smiling, but also not scowling. Graham inhaled a deep breath and turned his focus to Elias. "I am hopelessly in love with your sister, Elias. And I aim to ensure she knows that every day of our lives. But I don't fault you for feeling that I am not worthy of her love, and I hold no animosity towards you."

Neither spoke again for a few moments, allowing the understanding to hang between them.

Graham touched the back of his hand to Diana's cheek. Her eyes remained closed and her breathing was steady. "I will give you some time with her and will send Lydia up to you."

Elias nodded in appreciation, unable to speak. Graham kissed her brow and rose from the bed. He rejoined the group in the drawing room, sending Lydia to join Elias as he promised. He took a chair near the fire and let his head crash into his hands. His shoulders shook from the emotion fighting to escape his body.

It wasn't long before Matt approached and knelt before him. "Graham, she's going to be all right. I know it."

Graham inhaled a deep breath. He raised his head and locked eyes with Matt. "She doesn't believe that I love her. She thinks that is just another lie, and I only have myself to blame for that."

"So you'll tell Diana when she wakes up. She's going to wake up, friend. Plus, it's clear to anyone that she loves you, too."

Graham gave Matt a small smile. "You're truly the best of friends, you know."

"I know. And I'll be the best uncle to all the babies you two shall have." Matt patted his friend on the shoulder and rose to a standing position.

"Excuse me, I believe you are forgetting someone." Graham hadn't realized that Elias and Lydia were back. Elias occupied the chair across from him. He looked around and assumed Hudson and Hannah were sitting with Diana now.

Matt laughed. "You'll be the serious uncle who teaches them how to do all the proper things. I'll be the fun uncle."

Graham's heart ached as he thought about their children, whose birth might never come to pass. He longed to hold a little version of Diana with her long, blonde curls and blue eyes. She had to come back to him. He would grovel at her feet every day until she forgave him.

Hudson and Hannah returned to the drawing room, and Hannah rushed to Lydia's arms, crying on her shoulder.

Elias and Hudson remained in the chairs across from Graham, both staring at the fire. Graham stared back at the floor in front of him, losing himself again in his thoughts. Willing for them to have a chance at a future together.

Graham thought about Diana laying upstairs without him, and all he wanted to do was sit by her. "It is getting late. I'm going to sit with Diana for the night."

Elias pinched the bridge of his nose. "Please alert me to any change, no matter what time."

Graham nodded in agreement. He turned and left for Diana's chamber. He relieved Mary for the evening, closing the door behind her. For the first time since he found her in the park, he was alone with his wife.

Graham sat in the chair next to her bed and stared at her. His heart hurt with longing to have her awake and talking to him. Even if all she wanted to do was yell at him, he'd be happy to let her as long as she was well. He leaned forward and took her hand in his. "My sweet Diana. Come back to me, please. I love you so much. I don't want to be here without you, sweetheart."

The hours ticked by as Graham continued to hold vigil by Diana's bed. He sat in the same chair, holding onto her hand, feeling the most helpless and useless he'd ever been. He promised anyone listening to his pleas that he would trade his life for hers if it came down to it.

Graham could see the light growing brighter in the room, making the sky a soft orange outside the window. It reminded him of his days of taking Midnight for sunrise rides back at his home. Once Diana was well, they would watch sunrises together from their country home. He vowed he would never keep a single thing from her again. She was the one who possessed his entire heart.

Graham thought he felt her fingers move under his hand. He shot forward in his chair. He looked between her face and her fingers. Had he imagined it? Graham watched, holding his breath and silently begging for movement. For any sign that she would wake.

Her fingers moved again. "Graham?" Her voice came out in a whisper. "Graham?"

CHAPTER SEVENTEEN

Diana

DIANA WASN'T SURE where she was. Her head hurt a little. All she knew was that she wanted Graham. Where was Graham?

"I'm here, sweetheart." She felt movement on the bed next to her, and then she could see him. Well, mostly. Her vision was still fuzzy.

Diana gave him a weak smile. "Graham, what happened?"

The sound of her husband's rich baritone might have made her swoon if she had been standing. "You fell from your horse, sweetheart. Please lie still. I must send for the doctor."

Graham must have reached for the bell pull, because Mitchell entered the room. She could hear Graham's instruction. "Send for the doctor immediately. Alert Lord Snowdon that her ladyship is awake."

Papa? How long had she been asleep? Graham leaned to where she could see him. "My papa is here?"

"No, darling. Your brother. He stayed here last night. He sat with you for a while with Lydia."

After a few minutes, her eyesight returned to normal, and she could see Graham clearly now. She saw an awful bruising on Graham's cheek. She touched it gently with the tips of her fingers. "What happened to your face, Graham? Who hurt you?"

"I will tell you everything after the doctor has seen you, my love, I promise."

Memories of the events before her accident came flooding back to her. She cringed and tears formed in her eyes. "Elias hit you, didn't he?"

Graham wiped away a single tear from her eye with his thumb. "You have my word that all will be explained. But first, we need to confirm that you are all right."

Elias burst into the room. "Diana? You are awake?" Lydia was on his heels.

"I'm fine, brother. Just a bit of a headache."

Lydia clasped her hand. "You gave us quite the scare, dearest."

"If I recall correctly, I must decide if I'm to hear my husband out. If my brother can keep his fists under control." She gave a pointed stare to Elias.

Elias spoke next in the most apologetic tone. "I believe we may better understand each other. I hope you will give him a chance to explain."

Diana couldn't believe her ears when she heard her brother's forgiving response.

"I already told her that the explanation can wait until after the doctor visits." Graham still held onto her other hand. She needed to feel his touch. It was what was grounding her and keeping her calm. Because she loved him. And he was the one person that she had come to need more than anyone.

Mitchell entered the room, with the doctor behind him. "I hear her ladyship is awake. Can everyone step back for a moment so I can complete my exam? I'll allow you to stay if you can remain quiet."

Everyone nodded and lined up together against the wall, watching and waiting. The doctor talked to Diana, asking her questions to test her memory. He checked her hearing and her eyes. He examined her again for any bruising or areas hurt from the impact of the fall.

The doctor closed his bag and smiled at Diana. "You are a most fortunate lady. You have a large bruise that formed on your shoulder, but your range of motion is good. I don't think there will be a lasting injury. Her cognition appears normal and no concern for her memory. Her eyesight and hearing are normal. I will give directions to your maid for what to include in your tisane to help with the headache. Otherwise, you should be just fine."

He shifted his focus to Graham. "I want her to rest in bed for a few days and then she can ease into her usual activities."

Graham leaped forward and hugged the man. "Thank you so much."

"You are quite welcome. I'll meet with her maid now and have her bring up the tisane. Send for me if you need me, but I think she will recover nicely."

Elias patted the man on the back, and the doctor departed.

Graham sat on the bed beside Diana, taking her hand again. "I was so afraid that I had lost you. Thank you for coming back to me." She could see the tears forming in his sparkling green eyes, and she longed to soothe his pain.

Diana looked at Elias and Lydia. "Might I have a moment alone with my husband?"

The couple nodded in understanding. "Of course, sister. We will ensure you are not disturbed." They left and shut the door behind them.

"I shouldn't have run away. I should have given you a chance to explain. I just love you so much that when I found out what you were hiding, I feared that all of this had been in my head. That you'd never felt anything for me."

"You love me?" Graham asked, genuine surprise and hope in his expression.

Diana's eyes filled with tears. "Of course I love you, you impossible man. That's what makes this all so much worse. I gave you my heart, my trust, everything, and you—"

"I know." Graham's voice broke as he shifted closer on the

bed, taking both her hands in his. "Diana, I need you to hear me. Truly hear me. Not just the words, but everything I should have told you from the beginning."

His thumbs stroked over her knuckles. "Please, sweetheart. After this, if you want me to leave forever, I will. But you deserve the complete truth."

Diana nodded slightly, and Graham drew in a shaky breath.

"I have always wanted to marry for love. I swore that would be the only reason I married. When I inherited the title, I also inherited forty-five thousand pounds of debt from my cousin. And I refused to marry to resolve the matter, even though that was what others suggested that I should do."

She watched him intently, seeing the truth in his eyes.

"The debt was to a man named Rothwell who…" Graham's jaw clenched. "Who threatened to hurt you if I didn't pay. Not just hurt you, Diana. He offered to reduce my debt if I would let him…" Then he shook.

"Graham—"

"I hit him for even suggesting it. And then he said if I didn't pay on time, he would make me watch while he—" Graham clenched his jaw and quavered, "I couldn't let that happen. I will die before I let anyone hurt you."

Tears welled in her eyes. "Why didn't you tell me?"

"Because I'm a coward," he admitted without hesitation, "Because I was ashamed. Because I wanted so desperately to be the man you thought I was—worthy of you, capable of protecting you, not some son of libertine drowning in debt."

Graham released her hands and stood, pacing beside the bed as the words poured out of him. "But mostly because I was terrified. The moment I saw you in that ballroom, Diana, something inside me changed and became yours. And it's not just your beauty, though God knows you continue to take my breath away. It was like my soul knew yours. And when we were caught in that compromising position, while I hadn't planned it, there was a part of me that was elated. Because it meant you would be mine. The only plan I had was to pay that blasted debt and then court you."

He turned back to her, his green eyes bright with unshed tears. "And then…I fell in love with you. Truly, madly, completely in love. The way you challenge me, the way you laugh, the brilliant way your mind works when you're analyzing those ledgers. The way you trusted me enough to give yourself to me so completely. And I knew—I knew I didn't deserve any of it."

Graham dropped to his knees beside the bed, looking up at her with complete vulnerability. "I told myself I was protecting you by keeping the truth from you. But I was also protecting myself. From your disappointment. From the possibility that you would realize I'm not the man you deserve. From the fear that you would think the worst of me and that I would have tricked you into this marriage."

Tears were streaming down her cheeks. She wanted to grab him and hold him close and tell him that he loved him. But she knew he needed to finish speaking the words. Only then could they finally put the whole matter behind them forever.

"I used your dowry because Rothwell's threats were escalating. He came to our home, Diana. He was in our house and he was following me. And the things he said… I couldn't risk him getting anywhere near you. So yes, I used the money. I betrayed your trust in the worst possible way because I was too proud and too afraid to simply tell you the truth."

Graham reached for her hand again, pressing it to his cheek. "I used your knowledge to determine which properties to sell. I told countless half-truths, kept things from you, used our passion to distract you when you asked questions. I did everything wrong, Diana. Everything. And I am so deeply, desperately sorry."

He drew a long breath and stared back at her. "But please know this…nothing that grew between us was a lie. Not the way I touched you, not the way I looked at you, not a single moment of what we've shared in our bed or out of it. I love you with a depth that terrifies me. You own every piece of my heart, my soul, my very being. You have since that first rain-soaked kiss in the gazebo, and you will until I draw my last breath. Even if you can never forgive me or feel the same."

"I do forgive you, Graham," she said, unable to stand for him to continue to blame himself.

"The property in Devon is expected to close in a week or so. Every penny of your dowry will be returned, plus interest. The sale will be enough to ensure you can complete all of the enhancements across the other estates."

He raked his hand through his hair, and it was quite disheveled. He was gorgeous. And the good man she knew in her heart that he was. Even when he was being a dolt.

"You're right," Diana said, shifting on the bed so she sat up straighter. "You did everything wrong. You lied, you manipulated, you treated me like a child who couldn't handle the truth. You broke my trust."

His head fell and his shoulders slumped.

"But you're wrong about one thing," she continued. "I don't deserve better than you. I deserve you—the real you. The man who gave me my first horse. The man who made me feel like I was the most beautiful and desired woman in the whole of England. The man who loves me enough to do whatever it takes to keep me safe. That is who you are. And that is the man I deserve."

His eyes glistened from unshed tears, as he came to sit by her on the bed.

"I fell in love with you, Graham. Not some version that must be perfect all the time, but you."

She wrapped her arms around his neck and pulled him closer. "I love you. But if you ever," Diana gave him her most pointed look, "ever keep something from me again, if you ever try to protect me by lying to me, I will make you regret it for the rest of your days. I am your wife, your partner, your equal. Not some delicate flower who needs to be sheltered from the truth."

"I know," Graham whispered. "You're the strongest person I know. Stronger than I could ever be."

"We are stronger together," Diana said, capturing his cheeks in her hands. "I love you. Desperately. Even when you're being an impossible, overprotective fool."

And she wouldn't hesitate to tell him if he played the part of a fool again.

CHAPTER EIGHTEEN
Diana

DIANA RELISHED HAVING her husband by her side for the past two days while she had to mostly stay in bed. Graham saw to her every comfort. Her friends came to visit her and kept her company or she saw to various correspondence the few times she could convince Graham to go and stretch his legs.

But as she watched another day dawn, she had just about as much as she could stand of looking at the same four walls. And her confinement only made her long to go riding with Luna again. Graham was worried that she wouldn't want to continue her lessons after her fall, but she loved riding too much to give it up. Although she agreed she wouldn't take off on her own again without Graham.

Graham promised that some of her next lessons would include learning to handle a variety of stops and ways to respond to situations that could occur, so she would be better prepared if something ran out in front of her again. But it would be a couple weeks before she could attempt to ride again.

Graham stirred next to her. "Are you awake already?"

"I am eager to leave our room today, just like you promised, and feel a bit more normal. Plus, I enjoy watching you sleep." She brushed his hair back from his brow and placed a gentle kiss on it.

"I agreed to tea in the drawing room, and I shall carry you

there. If you try to do too much, I'm hauling you right back upstairs."

Diana giggled and placed a quick kiss on her husband's bare shoulder. "Perhaps that is what I wish for you to do."

Her efforts to talk her husband into bending the rules a bit and thoroughly bedding her had failed since he was adamant she needed to be fully recovered. He was terrified of losing her, and she appreciated he loved her so much that he wouldn't risk her well-being.

He gave her bottom a playful swat, then kissed her nose. "Don't make me change my mind."

"It's too late now," Diana teased. "I told Lady Harrowby she could join today when I wrote to thank her for the flowers. She's been insistent on wanting to visit when I was well. If you want to tell the dragon she is no longer welcome for tea, be my guest."

Graham shuddered. "You have me there. But I'll be keeping my eye on you."

"I promise that I will be good the entire time," she shifted so her lips brushed his ear. "And then I'm going to convince you to be quite bad."

He groaned in response. "You don't play fair. A man can only take so much." He pulled her to him and pressed his lips to hers, slipping his tongue inside when she parted for him.

And just when she thought he might cave, he broke the kiss. "I think you are in need of a good breakfast to start the day. Then we will get you dressed so you can break free. I'm a man of my word."

She watched like a hungry lioness as he moved from the bed. She had memorized every single one of his muscles and couldn't wait to touch and kiss each one.

But that would have to wait. Diana conceded and wrapped her dressing robe around herself and tied it tight. "Can we eat together by the fire?"

"You know I can deny you nothing."

"Well, that is just not true." She smirked at him and walked to the settee close to the fire to take her seat.

"I can deny you nothing that I don't fear will harm your well-being." He returned her smirk. "I do believe you are close to being back to your normal self now. We'll see how your energy level is today when you are up and about. I'll be staying close to you all day to ascertain for myself."

"Is that a promise, my love?" She winked at him.

He groaned again. "You are going to be the death of me, darling. Although, I do have a little something in mind after you are properly fed, and I think you will quite enjoy it."

The breakfast trays arrived, and they ate together by the warmth of the fire. She poured tea for each of them, and they chatted about some of the latest estate reports from Wilms. The property in Devon had sold and as soon as Diana was well, they were going to take their trip to begin implementing her changes.

Once they had finished eating, Graham pulled Diana to stand. "Close your eyes."

She did as he asked and he kissed her forehead. He laced his fingers with hers and pulled her with him. He positioned her where he wanted her. "Open your eyes."

Diana did as he commanded, and before her the tub was filled with hot water and two bath sheets on the hanger. She could smell the scent from the oils that had been placed in the water.

Graham pulled at the sash of her dressing robe to remove it. "I thought you might appreciate a proper bath." He dropped her robe on the floor and pulled her night rail over her head.

"Only if you are joining me." Diana slipped his banyan over his shoulders, and it fell to the floor. Graham scooped her up and cradled her in his arms as he stepped over the side of the tub and sat down in the water, settling her between his legs with her back leaned against his chest just as they had done many times.

Graham reached for the soap and kissed Diana's neck while he lathered up her body. He tenderly washed her from head to toe, including her hair. She closed her eyes and enjoyed the care and tenderness that he lavished upon her body.

Needing to touch him, Diana shifted so that she faced him, running her hands along his body, paying special attention to his thighs. She let the back of her hands brush his fully erect cock. Do it for longer the more he groaned.

"You're playing with fire, wife."

"I am quite aware."

Graham pulled her closer. His cock was erect and pressed between them. "Perhaps I can make a small concession if it should please my wife."

Diana moved so that she rubbed her sensitive core against his cock. "It would very much please your wife."

He moaned her name and trailed his fingers down her thigh until his thumb found her pearl. She leaned her head back and arched her chest towards him, inviting him to take her nipples into his mouth. Diana reached her hand between them, wrapping her fingers around his length. She stroked him, and he shifted his hips to meet the pressure of her hand.

It didn't take long and she was crying out from her climax just as Graham's shaft had become hard as steel, pulsing in her hand. After the pleasure subsided, she collapsed against her husband's chest.

"Are you all right, love?" Graham kissed her brow.

"I'm wonderful. But I'm never bathing without you again."

CHAPTER NINETEEN
Graham

GRAHAM HELPED DIANA to the settee in the drawing room, arranging cushions behind her back despite her protests that she was perfectly capable of sitting on her own. The bruise on her shoulder might be fading, but the memory of finding her unconscious in the park still haunted him.

"Graham, truly, I'm well," Diana said, though her smile indicated she didn't actually mind being fussed over.

"Humor me," he murmured, pressing a kiss to her temple before straightening. "Mother, would you like more tea?"

Augusta looked up from her embroidery. "Yes, dear. But let me tend to that so you can continue to hover over your wife."

Diana released a stream of giggles. "He's a mess."

"Can you blame me?" Graham settled on the settee beside Diana as his mother prepared them each a cup of tea.

"I find it rather endearing," Diana said, accepting the cup Augusta offered. "Though I draw the line at being carried everywhere like an invalid."

Before he could respond, Mitchell appeared in the doorway. "Lady Harrowby has arrived for tea, my lady."

Diana straightened in her seat. "Oh wonderful! I invited her yesterday. Well, she practically invited herself, but we have hardly been making social appearances since we married. It will be good for the gossips to know all is well in our marriage." She glanced at Augusta. "You'll adore her. She's rather formidable and has the entire ton by the ear."

Graham noticed his mother had gone very still, and her embroidery fell across her lap. The color had drained from her face entirely. "Mother? Are you well?"

Augusta set down her needlework, her fingers trembling visibly. "I… forgive me. I'm quite well."

Lady Harrowby swept into the room in her characteristic fashion, adorned in deep purple with her signature elaborate turban. "My dear Diana, how wonderful to see you up and about. I've been worried sick since I heard—"

She stopped mid-sentence, her sharp gaze landing on Augusta. Augusta's teacup rattled against its saucer as she set it down with unsteady hands.

For a long moment, neither woman spoke. Then Augusta's voice came out as barely a whisper. "Hello, Mama."

Graham's own cup clattered to the floor, spilling all over the carpets. "Mama?" He looked between the two women, his mind struggling to make sense of what he'd heard. "Lady Harrowby is your mother?"

Diana gasped softly beside him, her hand finding his.

Lady Harrowby stood frozen in the doorway, her usual commanding presence wavering. Tears gathered in her eyes, though she fought to maintain her composure. "Augusta." Her voice broke slightly on the name. "My daughter. You look… you look well."

"I am well." Augusta rose slowly, as if any sudden movement might shatter the moment. "I have been well for many years."

Graham found his voice, though it came out harder than he intended. "Someone needs to explain what's happening. Now." His commanding tone cut through the emotion in the room. "Lady Harrowby, you're telling me you're my grandmother?"

"Yes." Lady Harrowby's gaze never left her daughter, though her hands shook as she removed her gloves. "Though I only learned of your existence after you inherited. I didn't know where my daughter was, but a man I knew who oversees the transfer of titles saw my daughter's name for your parentage. Even your mother's friends here in town would never tell me a thing about what had become of her. Almost thirty years, Augusta, without so much as a word."

Augusta's chin lifted, and Graham glanced between the pair, uncertain to make of what he was hearing.

"I had to leave."

"Because of love? All that you said in your letter was that you were going to marry another. That you chose him over the Duke of Yorkshire." Lady Harrowby moved closer, raising her voice, though remaining even. "But I never understood why. There were whispers of you being alone with some man, but your father and I could have managed the scandal."

Graham sat down heavily, his mind reeling. His mother had been intended for a duke? She had run away from her family and ended up with his father. None of this made any sense. "The Duke of Yorkshire, Mama?"

Augusta let out a bitter laugh, though tears had begun to flow. "Is that what you thought all these years? That I chose Graham's father out of some romantic notion?" She pressed a hand to her chest, as if she were gathering courage. "Oh, Mama. You never knew the truth."

Diana squeezed Graham's hand, grounding him as everything he'd believed about his family began to shift.

"Then tell me," Lady Harrowby demanded, though her careful composure was beginning to crack. "Tell me why you threw away your future, and why you ran from your family. Why did you let me wonder what had happened to you all of these years?"

Augusta's hands twisted in her lap. She stared at them for a long moment before speaking. "The Duke of Yorkshire..." She paused as tears welled in her eyes. "That night at the Pembridge ball, he cornered me in the library. He'd been drinking heavily. He said things... did things..."

Every part of Graham's body tensed. Beside him, Diana made a soft sound of distress.

"I refused him and he became enraged. The duke tore at my bodice, and pressed against the bookshelf. He tried to…" Augusta couldn't finish the sentence, her voice catching. "I managed to break free from him, and I ran. I ran as fast as I could through the garden and then out into the street. Charles—Graham's father— was on horseback and saw me there. He…"

Lady Harrowby's expression had shifted to one of horror, and her eyes had become watery. "And he saved you?"

"He stopped to help me, and I couldn't speak. I just cried in his arms. But my dress was torn, and he surmised what must have occurred." Augusta's tears flowed freely now. "But someone saw us, when Charles was comforting me. They called me a lightskirt and ran back into the ball."

"Why didn't you tell me?" Lady Harrowby's voice was anguished. "I could have—"

"Could have what?" Augusta's voice grew stronger, anger mixing with her pain. "Forced me to marry my attacker? You were so set on the match, so proud that a duke wanted me. You kept saying we could smooth over the scandal, that the duke would still have me despite the gossip. I couldn't bear to tell you what he'd truly done. I was so ashamed."

Graham sat in stunned silence, watching his entire understanding of his father reshape itself. The man he'd thought was a callous seducer had actually been a hero. His parents' marriage hadn't been born of lust and scandal, but of protection and desperate necessity.

"So Father married you to save your reputation," Graham said slowly and hoarsely.

Augusta nodded, wiping her eyes with a trembling hand. "He was honorable. He knew I'd be ruined otherwise, that no decent man would have me after such gossip. But we never loved each other, not in that way. We were grateful to each other, respectful, but we remained strangers bound by circumstance. When he began seeking comfort elsewhere..." She shrugged helplessly. "I couldn't blame him entirely. We were both trapped in a marriage neither of us had chosen."

"But he saved you," Diana said softly. "Whatever came after, in that moment, he saved you."

"Yes." Augusta looked at Graham, her eyes pleading for understanding. "Your father wasn't the villain you believed him to be, my son. He was flawed, yes. The marriage was unhappy, yes. But he wasn't evil. And he gave me you. He did his best in an impossible situation."

The emotion threatened to overtake him. All these years of hating his father's behavior, of fearing he'd inherit some inescapable corruption from the man, and he was able to see the man much differently.

Lady Harrowby finally closed the distance to her daughter, her movements uncertain. "May I?"

Augusta nodded, and Lady Harrowby pulled her into her arms. "My dear, brave girl. My foolish, courageous daughter. If I had known... If that monster Yorkshire weren't already dead, I would promise that I would kill him myself."

Augusta clung to her mother, sobbing harder than he'd ever seen. "I'm sorry, Mama. I'm so sorry I stayed away."

"No." Lady Harrowby pulled back, cupping her daughter's face with both hands. "I'm sorry. I should have suspected that something was amiss. Should have protected you better. Should have known you wouldn't throw everything away without reason. I failed you."

Graham stood frozen, watching his mother and grandmother embrace. Everything he had believed about his family, about himself, had been turned upside down. He wasn't entirely different from his father in some ways. They were both fierce protectors, and ended up in marriages based on circumstances.

"Graham." Diana's gentle voice drew his attention. She was looking up at him with understanding and love. "Are you all right?"

Was he? His father was still flawed, and had still hurt his mother with his infidelities. But now Graham understood it differently. Two people trapped in a marriage built on gratitude and obligation rather than love, both suffering in their own ways. That could have been the story for him and Diana if things hadn't have worked out much differently.

"I don't know," he admitted, his voice rough.

Diana stood, wavering slightly, and he immediately steadied her. "Your father saved your mother," she whispered where only he could hear. "Whatever came after, in that moment, he chose to protect her at great personal cost. That matters."

She was right. It did matter. It changed everything Graham had believed about himself, about the legacy he carried.

"We're quite the pair, aren't we?" Graham murmured, thinking of their own marriage born from scandal. "History repeats itself."

"No." Diana's voice was firm. "We're writing our own story. We found love despite the circumstances. That's what makes us different."

Lady Harrowby approached them, Augusta at her side, both women's faces still streaked with tears. "Graham," his grandmother said, and the word held such weight. "My grandson. I've wanted to acknowledge you since the moment I realized who you were."

"Why didn't you?"

"I thought Augusta had... well, I thought you knew and chose not to acknowledge me as your family."

Graham looked at his mother. "You never told me who your parents were. I assumed they were dead."

"I was wrong for that," Augusta said, cupping his cheek. "The girl I was—Lady Augusta Harrowby—she ceased to exist the night I fled with your father. I became someone else. Someone smaller, quieter. Someone hidden from the world."

"No more hiding," Lady Harrowby declared. "No more separation. We're family, all of us."

"There's more," Augusta said, looking at her son with hesitation. "About your father. Things you should know, if you're ready to hear them."

Graham tensed, but nodded. He wasn't certain he could stomach any more revelations at present. "Tell me."

"He tried to love me. In the beginning, he truly tried. But I couldn't..." She paused for a moment and then released a long sigh. "After what the duke had attempted, I couldn't bear to be touched. Not for a long time. By the time I could, too much distance had grown between us. We were strangers sharing a house."

"The other women..."

"Started after you were born. He had you as his heir to the business. After that, we lived separate lives under the same roof. It wasn't what either of us wanted, but it was what we could manage." Augusta held his chin as she looked up into his eyes. "But you, my dear boy. You were the one good thing to come from it all. He loved you. Never doubt that."

Graham thought of his own marriage, of how differently things had gone despite the similar beginning. He and Diana had chosen each other every day since their wedding, and had built something real from an impossible situation.

"I wish you had told me sooner."

"I probably should have, and for that I hope you can forgive me. I thought I was protecting you from the burden of knowing who I truly was. I never thought you'd end up with a title and thrust into society. But seeing the happiness you have found with Diana, I can see that this is where you were always meant to be."

Diana stepped beside him and he put his arm around her, needing to hold her close.

Lady Harrowby cleared her throat, and clapped her hands together. "I think we are in need of a fresh pot of tea after this reunion." She wiped the tears away from her cheeks. "And then, Augusta, you're coming home with me. We have much to catch up on."

"Mama, I couldn't—"

"Nonsense. Graham has his wife to look after. You'll stay with me for a few days at least." Lady Harrowby's tone brooked no argument. "I'm not letting you out of my sight so quickly after finally finding you again."

Graham saw the yearning in his mother's eyes. "Go," he urged. "Diana and I will be fine. You should have this time with her."

Augusta hugged him tightly. "You've inherited the best of your father's traits. I hope you can come to see that."

As Graham watched his mother and grandmother settle together on the settee with their hands clasped. The anger he'd carried toward his father didn't disappear entirely, but it transformed into something more complex. It was more like understanding, perhaps even pity.

And for the first time in his life, Graham didn't feel the weight of his father's perceived failures pressing down on him. He was free to be the man, the husband, the son, and grandson, and, he hoped, one day the father he chose to be.

Diana leaned into him, and he pressed a kiss to the top of her head.

"I love you," he whispered to his wife. "And my love is forever."

Diana's smile was radiant. "I love you too, my unexpected earl. I'm thankful we were both wandering in the garden that night."

As Mitchell brought in a fresh cart for their refreshment, conversation between Augusta and his grandmother shifted to stories and reminiscing. Graham held his wife and marveled at how truth could change everything.

His father hadn't been a villain. His mother hadn't been weak. They'd simply been two people caught in an impossible situation who'd done their best with what they had.

He and Diana would do better. They already were.

EPILOGUE

Graham

Two Weeks Later
Kent Estate

DIANA GUIDED LUNA along the ridge overlooking their primary estate in Kent. The mare responded to her slightest touch, and Diana reveled in the freedom of being back atop her horse and the opportunity to ride across the countryside in a way she couldn't have done back in London.

"Getting rather confident, aren't we?" Graham called from beside her on Midnight, his green eyes sparkling with amusement and a hint of pride.

"Confident enough to race you back to the stables," Diana challenged, already turning Luna toward home.

"Diana, wait—"

But she was already urging Luna into a canter, laughing as she heard Graham curse behind her before Midnight's hoofbeats thundered in pursuit. Racing Luna sent excitement coursing through her, with the morning air crisp against her cheeks.

They were nearly to the fence line when the queasiness hit.

Diana pulled Luna to an abrupt stop, her stomach roiling. She pressed a hand to her mouth, willing the sensation to pass.

"Diana?" Graham was beside her instantly, with Midnight dancing anxiously beneath him. "What's wrong?"

"I need to—" She didn't finish, sliding from Luna's back and stumbling to the nearby hedgerow where she lost what little breakfast she'd managed.

Graham was off his horse and at her side in an instant, steadying her with a supportive hand on her back. "Sweetheart, what's happened? Should I send for the doctor?"

Diana accepted the handkerchief he offered, wiping her mouth with shaking hands. "It's nothing. Perhaps I rode too hard after eating."

His brows drew together as he studied her face, one hand coming to rest against her forehead. "You're not feverish. But Diana, this has happened the past few mornings now."

They looked at each other in silence. Diana watched confusion flicker across Graham's features before his eyes slowly widened with understanding.

"Could it be...?" His voice came out uncertain, as if he hardly dared to voice the thought.

Diana's hand moved instinctively to her abdomen. "It's certainly possible. And given our enthusiasm for certain activities."

Graham's entire expression transformed, joy and wonder replacing concern. "Our child," he whispered, his hand covering hers. "Diana, we might have a precious babe."

"We don't know for certain yet," she said softly, though her heart was already racing with the possibility.

He helped her to sit on a fallen log, kneeling before her and taking her hands in his. "How are you feeling now? Better?"

"Much better. The morning air helps." She squeezed his hands. "We should walk the horses back."

Diana stood slowly, grateful when the world remained steady. "Perhaps we will share our suspicions with your mama and grandmama."

Although given the way they'd watched her since they had arrived, they might already have ascertained the same.

"Of course." Graham helped her back onto Luna, his hands lingering on her waist. "Though if you're feeling unwell again—"

"I'm fine," she assured him, though she appreciated his concern. "Just... perhaps no more races until we know for certain."

They rode back slowly, side by side, Graham's hand occasionally reaching over to touch hers where it rested on Luna's neck. Once they reached the stables, he carefully lifted her down.

Hand in hand, they walked toward the house. Her mind raced with thoughts of hope that she carried their first child.

As they entered through the garden door, Diana could hear the women chatting in the morning room.

"There you are!" Augusta's voice carried down the hallway. "We were beginning to wonder if you'd ridden to London and back."

They found Augusta and Lady Harrowby together in the morning room already settled with tea. They appeared almost as if they had never been apart. Diana took her seat on the open settee nearby.

"Mother, I hope you're planning to stay through the end of the month," Graham said, settling beside Diana. "Diana's been working with Crawford on the winter preparations, and I think you'd enjoy seeing her improvements in action."

Diana reached for the plate of small cakes beside the tea service, her mouth watering at the sight. "Lemon cakes," she said with satisfaction, selecting one. "I've been craving these all morning."

Graham chuckled beside her. "Don't go sharing those cakes with just anyone. They are a weapon in the wrong hands."

"I've already captured my earl," Diana replied, giggling as she took a bite.

"And you didn't require cake, my love." Graham's hand found hers automatically.

Lady Harrowby cleared her throat, but she wore an approving grin.

Diana swatted her husband's arm playfully and focused on the women. "How long are you both planning to stay?"

"We aren't in a rush to depart," Augusta replied, reaching for the teapot. "Besides, Diana might need—"

She stopped abruptly, her gaze moving between Diana and

Graham before focusing on her tea.

"Need what?" Diana asked carefully, though she had a feeling she knew where this was leading.

"Well," Lady Harrowby started, "We couldn't help but notice you've been rather pale these past few mornings. And Graham has been hovering even more than usual, if such a thing is possible."

Diana allowed her hopes to rise. If the women also suspected, then it seemed it would be even more likely.

"We... that is, we think it's possible..." Diana glanced at Graham, who nodded in agreement. "But it's too early to be certain."

Augusta's eyes filled with tears as she looked between Graham and Diana. "A grandchild," she repeated softly. "Oh, my dear children. How wonderful if it's true."

She rose, reaching for Diana to pull her into a tight embrace. "I'm certain your mother would have been so proud to see you married and settled. And if you are indeed expecting..." She paused, obviously overcome by emotion.

Graham rose and placed his hand on the small of her back. "I keep thinking Father would have been amazed to see how everything worked out as well."

"He would have been a devoted grandfather," Augusta said with certainty. "For all his faults, he loved children. He used to say that babies were proof that hope exists in the world."

Diana felt the tears coming as she imagined her husband holding their babe in his arms, and all of their family and friends there in support.

Augusta returned to her mother. The two women began discussing possibilities and preparations, and Graham leaned closer to Diana, his lips brushing her ear.

"How are you feeling? Truly?"

Diana considered the question carefully. "Tired. Queasy in the mornings. And rather emotional, it seems." She paused, wiping tears from her eyes. "But also... hopeful. Frightened, but hopeful."

Graham's hand moved to rest gently over her still-flat stomach. "Whatever happens, we'll face it together."

"I know," Diana said, covering his hand with hers. "Though if I am expecting, you cannot spend the entire time treating me as if I might break. Promise me."

Graham's smile was rueful. "I'll try. Though you must promise to tell me if you need anything. Anything at all."

"I promise."

Graham lifted their joined hands to press a kiss to her knuckles. "We've built something beautiful, haven't we?"

"More beautiful than I ever could have imagined."

And it was only going to get better.

The End

Dearest Reader

Thank you for taking the time to immerse yourself into my Regency world! I hope you enjoyed this spicy read from my Romancing the Ton series! I hope you will keep reading this amazing series with some of my absolute favorite characters!

I am so thankful for all my readers and would appreciate it if you would leave an honest review on sites like Amazon, Goodreads, BookBub, etc.! Also, I'd love to stay in touch, so please visit christinadianebooks.com to join my mailing list and receive a free copy of *Only A Rake Will Do* (also connected to the group of friends in Romancing the Ton), and stay informed on upcoming releases, promotions, and current projects.

I hope all of you will follow me and get the latest happenings and info on releases from my historical romance friends on any of my socials:

- Website: christinadianebooks.com
- Substack: @christinadianeauthor
- The Desire Den Discord
- Instagram: @christinadianeauthor
- Facebook: christinadiane
- TikTok: @christinadianeauthor
- YouTube: @ChristinaDianeAuthor
- BlueSky: @christinadiane.bsky.social
- Twitter: @CDianeAuthor

- GoodReads: ChristinaDiane
- Follow Me on Amazon: Christina Diane
- Follow Me on BookBub: Christina Diane
- Join my Reader Group: The Swoonworthy Scoundrels Society [Facebook]
- Also hang out with me here: Society of Smut & Scandal [Facebook]
- And here: Wanton Wallflowers [Facebook]

Acknowledgments

There are so many incredible people—both new and longtime ride-or-dies—who have supported me on this wild writing journey. Authors, readers, friends, family, co-workers… you know who you are. I'd list every one of you if I had a few extra pages (and a really small font). Just know this: I adore you, and I'm endlessly grateful.

Steve: My husband, tech wizard, idea bouncer, chef, laundry hero, and all-around MVP. You believe in my big, bold dreams even when they sound like total chaos. Thank you for being my partner in every possible way. Love you, babe.

Dexter and Felix: My boys, my chaos gremlins, and the source of many laughs. You're excellent at distracting me mid-sentence, but you're also the inspiration behind some of the snarky sibling banter that sneaks into my books. One day you'll realize your mom writes smut… and I'll probably owe you both ice cream and therapy. Love you forever.

Rachel, Nina & Brittany: My mom, aunt, and sister—aka my built-in cheer squad. You've supported me through every high, low, and harebrained idea I've ever chased. You hold all my most embarrassing stories, so let's make sure you never talk to anyone without legal counsel present. I love you all dearly.

Erin: From the moment fate brought us together in the most unexpected way, we knew we were meant to be besties. Thank you for listening to every rant, dream, plot twist in life, and meltdown—and for always helping me find my way back to joy and clarity. You're pure magic.

Courtney: Fate handed me a twin flame in the author world. We literally finish each other's sentences (or just say the same thing) and have become legit besties. I can't wait for the day we meet in person. Thank you for our pretty much all day, every day chats, late-night idea storms, the pep talks, and all the chaos we've embraced together. We've got this, twinsie!

Morgan: The magic behind the scenes! You keep everything running, offer genius-level input, and somehow make it all feel easier and more fun. This book—and honestly, this business— wouldn't be the same without you. Thank you, thank you, thank you.

Bliss: Who knew a smutty follow train on Insta would bring me one of my dearest friendsies? Thank you for the endless texts, laughter, spicy scene brainstorming, feedback on my chaos, and all-around moral support. So lucky we found each other!

To my **ARC and Street Team:** Your love, feedback, and support make my heart full. Thank you for shouting about these stories from the rooftops—you make this adventure feel like a party I never want to leave.

To **Dragonblade Publishing:** Thank you for believing in me and my words. I'm so excited to grow alongside such a passionate and supportive team, and be among your esteemed group of authors.

And to all the amazing **author friends** and **influencers** I've met through social media: You're one of the best, most unexpected blessings of this entire journey. Thank you for the inspiration, the laughs, the advice—and most of all, for welcoming me into this magical community.

Meet the Author

Christina Diane is an award-winning, bestselling author who loves to write super spicy, fast-paced stories for the modern reader in the genres of historical romance and dark romance. Her historical romances are all set in the Regency era, with creative liberty taken within the historical setting to create a passionate, hot, intriguing story. Across all of her works, if you love combinations of high spice, witty banter, spirited heroines, forbidden romances, darker themes, and hot alpha men…then you are in for a treat! Because bad boys never go out of style!

She is a hybrid indie and traditionally published author with Dragonblade Publishing, Romance Cafe, and And You Press. She reads mostly spicy Regency romances and all shades of dark romances, as well as thrillers.

Christina lives in Northern Maine with her husband and two boys. When she is not writing or chasing after her family, she usually has a Kindle in her hand!

Her writing journey began at the age of nine when she created her own comic strip, Grizzly Grouch. In adulthood, she was a freelance writer for several years, mostly writing lifestyle pieces for blogs. She found that she couldn't stop thinking about stories and characters, so much that she had to get them on the page! Christina frequently has dreams of random character ARCs that go into a massive list of planned writings. She currently has more than ten series just waiting to be written!

Aside from her family, writing, and books, she loves Bridgerton, the Grinch, Jessica Rabbit, horror movies, Chucky dolls, cold brew, yoga, Hamilton, the color pink, and speaking in obscure quotes from movies and TV shows.

Christina loves chatting with her readers and talking about great reads, so please contact her on socials or christinadianebooks.com! She'd love to hear what you think about her books and what you'd love to see more of!

www.ingramcontent.com/pod-product-compliance
Lightning Source LLC
Chambersburg PA
CBHW060420310726
48976CB00003B/1135